THE METRIC CLOCK

The Adventures of Charles, Transforming a
Precocious Boy into a Young Man

PHILLIP B. CHUTE

Copyright © 1984 by Phillip Bruce Chute

First paperback edition November 2018

Book cover GermanCreative
Cover and inside illustrations by DJ Smith
Editing by Alice Wakefield

ISBN (paperback) 978-1-7328855-0-9

www.phillipbchute.com

Table of Contents

Prelude vi

SPRING

Chapter One
The Storm 1

Chapter Two
A Day at School 12

Chapter Three
The Spy 26

Chapter Four
The Contest 31

Chapter Five
Buttercups 42

SUMMER

Chapter Six
Going Fishing 52

Chapter Seven
Learning to Smoke 62

Chapter Eight
Muskrats 71

Chapter Nine
Excursion to the Marsh 79

Chapter Ten
The Harvest 90

FALL

Chapter Eleven
The Journey 97

Chapter Twelve
The Mountain Farm 103

Chapter Thirteen
The Hunt 112

Chapter Fourteen
Escape from the Wilderness 118

Table of Contents

Chapter Fifteen
Tom's Secret 124

Chapter Sixteen
The Apple War 131

Chapter Seventeen
Sweet Revenge 138

Chapter Eighteen
The Spy's Lair 146

WINTER

Chapter Nineteen
Turning Ten 156

Chapter Twenty
Gang War Again 161

Chapter Twenty-One
Holidays 168

The Metric Clock:
Postlude 172

About the Author 176

The Author's Other Works 177

Charles' Neighborhood

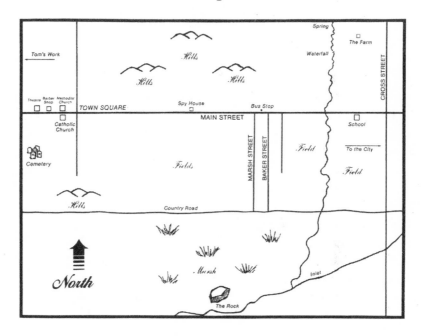

Prelude

Charlie Wallace had come home. Strong arms opened the car door and helped the small light-framed man into the crisp fall air. Greetings and a dozen outthrust hands from the men welcomed him back after his three-decade journey. He looked into the crowd of people and smiled back at them. 'So, this is what it's like to be away after all those years,' he thought, 'I thought they would forget me.' He felt out of place among the well-dressed people with the comfortable grey woolen sweater and casual slacks he had traveled in.

A slight, straw blonde woman of equal height, hearing the commotion, opened the front door of the house and rushed to greet him with open arms. Her appearance in a flowered cotton house dress and flowing long hair startled the crowd into silence. The church members who had not seen her before were awed by the large depthless azure blue eyes that dominated her simple countenance.

"Mary Anne," Charles spoke softly into her ear, "it's good to be home again." The smell of her perfumed neck and hair filled his senses making him aware how much he missed his wife.

The mob followed them into a house filled with vapors of fresh paint. The women headed directly for the kitchen. Shortly coffee, tea and hot rolls were being served. Charles settled into a worn leather chair terraced with cracks from years of use. One by one, and in couples, the people flowed by him exchanging introductions and greetings. They were fascinated by the man in his early fifties with creases around his eyes from frequent smiles while masking the sharpness of the deep brown eyes that were known to be intellectually critical yet propitious. Those eyes of endless curiosity and searching had become the analytical eyes of the Church all over the world. Charlie's Inquisition...was the term used to describe his tour of all the parishes to rebuild the infrastructure into a Church of Stone, not sticks and stones, as he would say. He was the architect of a new church, and to build a new some things must be torn down first. Charles was embarrassed and pleasantly defensive because he recognized no one. The afternoon wore on until suddenly Mary Anne was standing before him studying his face.

"You look awfully tired from the trip. I'll send everybody away. Haven't they been wonderful?" Then with a weary smile she went about the house quietly asking people to leave.

'I don't like what I see in his face,' she thought. 'The softness of his face is pale and creased with fatigue. His dark brown sensitive eyes, which I learned to love so much, and used to sparkle with energy, are clouded... not from age, but from the heart attack and the trip. I see his strength slipping away from him. Like the sand in an hourglass, soon it will be all drained away. How I used to lean on him all the years, never dreaming that one day he would need me in turn.'

After the front door closed a final time Mary Anne found Charles wandering about the living room running his right hand over the carved fireplace mantle as he walked past it.

"A craftsman carved this wood. I wish I could carve so well." Charles smiled a deep smile that creased the corners of his eyes as well as his mouth as he looked around the room filled with bookshelves and books from wall to wall.

"Mary Anne look at all these books! Where did they come from? Who lived here?"

Mary Anne put her arm around his waist and rested her head on his shoulder. Her blue eyes were weary from the advance trip to get the house ready for Charles. The day had capped a very long and eventful month. She handed him a capsule.

"Take this for the pain. I'm glad you like it here. The congregation got together to fix up this marvelous old Victorian house for us. Mrs. Dotson, the minister's wife, told me all about it. She said that somebody found out how much you love to read so they gathered up all the books you see in this room and built the bookcases. All the books are signed by the people who brought them. Perhaps they want you to know they read them or what they like to read. They also converted a downstairs room into a bedroom so you won't have to go up and down the stairs at night." She saw the glowing smile crowning his tired face.

"This place is beautiful. What a fine way to retire...with the love of all these strangers and you." He swallowed the capsule and ran his hand through thick fine white hair as he surveyed the room again. His hand rested on Mary Anne's shoulder.

"There must be thousands of books here. The parishioners must have emptied their houses of books for me. What a great thought...

deed. Now I receive payment from God by the people themselves...this house, the books, and God knows what else. We'll be happy here."

His eyes stopped at Mary Anne. The shadows under her eyes betrayed the fatigue. She also felt thin under his hand. "You're getting skinny. I'm the one who's sick, not you." He knew that she had been worried and would peck away at her food like a bird watching a cat in the distance.

Together they stood resting silently as the minutes ticked by. There was no need to speak of things understood and experienced over a lifetime. Two lives sharing the ultimate companionship through the years. In diurnal closeness there were many times when one of them would start to speak to the other and find no need because words were not required.

Shadows filled the lower pane of the front window as darkness approached. Mary Anne moved to a lamp which clicked loudly as it suddenly filled the room with light. Charles stood by the fireplace as she left for the kitchen. His eyes squinted in the brightness and opened again as dilated pupils adjusted. A heater fan started whirring away in the environs of the house.

Charles immersed himself in the events preceding the trip to the house. After the heart attack, although it was not considered severe by the doctors, he felt an ominous prescience that it was a warning. At first, he tried to discount the feeling that it was a signal of worse things to come but would wake up at night thinking that it must be a sign for him to slow down his energetic pace. His meteoric and demanding ascendance in the Church, like an express train rushing into the night without ever stopping or slowing down, sure of course and cadence forever, had taken its toll and he knew he had paid the price for his ambition at an early time in life. A desire to return to his childhood home grew from an occasional thought until it now became an obsession. Mary Anne had readily agreed. They needed a change of pace and a view of the past before this life was ended. 'I only hope', he thought, in his preoccupation with death, 'that she will not die with me. I cannot ask that of this woman who has stood by me all these years.'

"Mary Anne," he yelled after her into the other room, "I want to visit the waterfall tomorrow. And also, the buttercup field."

Mary Anne reappeared with a dish towel in hand. "Charles, I don't know what to tell you. I went to the Main Street last week, you know I spent my childhood there and yet I got lost, and," suddenly she stopped as tears came to her eyes as her voice wavered, "everything is gone."

Charles felt a wave of panic overcome him. He slowly edged himself into the leather chair. "Nonsense, Mary Anne, how could everything be gone. How could a waterfall disappear?"

"It's true, really Charles. The developers have piped the water away and built rows of houses where the waterfall and field used to be. Even the old schoolhouse is torn down. I drove round and round and couldn't find a trace of anything familiar."

Charles grew angry. Hidden emotions welled up from inside rushing out at the nearest person. He lashed out at Mary Anne without thinking. "Next you'll tell me that the Marsh Street Gang is gone too!"

Mary Anne started to say something but closed her mouth knowing he saw none of the Marsh Street Gang at the house today.

"I'll get some tea while you cool down," she said as she hurried safely into the kitchen.

Charles felt heat flow into his face. His hands gripped the arms of the chair. Then he slowly relaxed as his consciousness took charge. He started talking without knowing if she heard or not. Charles had to say what was on his mind and had obsessed him this past month since the heart attack.

"We came back for nothing. When I found out how sick I was I felt a great longing in my heart to return and see the places where we grew up. The most important thing in the world was to visit the place where I learned to love you and think about God and the good things of the earth. Instead, all we have found are more houses and people. I'm so glad that we had a chance to grow up in a beautiful place before it was destroyed. Pity the poor people who must grow up in a world devoid of nature."

Mary Anne returned with a bottle of red wine from the refrigerator. Beautifully cut lead crystal glasses appeared from a cabinet. She filled one and held it out to him, it caught a prismatic glint of color from the disappearing afternoon sun. Pulling a chair opposite him she set the bottle down on the table next to the lamp after filling her glass. She felt his anger. It was hers also.

"Charles, I know how you must feel. I was also looking forward to seeing the old places and things that we remember." She leaned forward and grasped his hand while looking into his dark eyes.

"Charles, maybe we expected too much. Most of the people we used to know are dead or moved away. Even the Marsh Street Gang is not around and nobody here has heard of them. Maybe it's better just to think of things as they were instead of expecting to find them the same again."

"You know Mary Anne, there was a year in my life, when I was about nine or ten years old, that was more important than anything or any time that I can remember."

"You mean except when you went into the ministry," Mary Anne corrected.

Charles sipped his wine and continued. "In that period somehow so many things happened to me that I felt I grew ten years older. I believe I fell in love with you during that year and started seriously thinking about God and the universe around us."

Mary Anne smiled. She relaxed as she began thinking about the purpose of their trip to the old town. 'I love the precious minutes when his time is free from the demands of the people of the Church. There may not be many more days to share with him. Time is precious and short. My love is coming full circle to its inception in this small town and place. I have always been thankful to live my life in his shadow and help him serve God. Somehow, I feel so attached to him that I am like a boat on the ocean going in and out with the tide. My life is his and he is the ocean. Lord, let me die with him. I don't want to be alone without him.' The enormity of the trip had suddenly encompassed her. A sip of wine brought her back to the conversation at hand.

"Remember how terrified we were of the spy?" she reminded him. "And the time the bees chased the gang home? I still remember the day the teacher stood you in the corner of the room because of that silly metric clock idea that you had." A great smile crossed her face as her blue eyes brightened.

Charles wistfully continued, "That time was a magical period. Everything was changing for me. It seems that I came alive and my senses sharpened. I learned to think for myself and the family and the Marsh Street Gang. So many good and bad things happened that made me aware of life. I wish, oh God, if I had one wish, that I could go back and relive the events that happened and become that child again."

He settled back into his chair. His eyes closed as he raced back in time.

Spring

Chapter One

The Storm

The little boy looked out the window from his tiny bedroom. It was late in the day but the sky was already darkened with the storm. He watched the snow race horizontally across the window and disappear in the oncoming night. Patches of snow piled up in the corners of the window to blow away and pile up again. The boy put his small hand on the window to feel the cold through the glass. He shivered, withdrawing to sit on his bed and watch from further back. 'Where does the cold come from?' he asked himself. 'Is it like darkness?'

He knew that darkness must be a million particles of almost invisible dark things that settled over the earth at night filling the sky until there was no more light. 'Where does the snow and cold come from?' he asked himself again. 'Is it stored up on the other side of the world someplace to shift around when God decides to move it?' He stared at the window in awe at the idea of all the cold, snow, and darkness descending on the helpless world and its people.

The wind outside howled with fury, causing the window to rattle. He shivered again and put his hands inside his pockets for warmth. The cold suddenly was too much for him and he went downstairs to his mother who was busy in the kitchen.

"Mother," he asked, "will there be school tomorrow? Can I stay home instead?" He watched her face for the reply he was looking forward to.

The young woman looked at her child, reaching out to pat his cowlick and push the hair away from his forehead. Then Rose turned back to the stove and told him what he expected to hear.

1

"This storm is a real Nor-easter blizzard and will probably shut everything down. I don't know how your father will get to work tomorrow morning if the roads aren't cleared for the busses. He changes busses three times to get to work in the city. Turn the radio on and sooner or later the school closings will be announced when they decide." Her face was long with concern about how Tom was going to get home with the snow deepening from the new storm.

Charles stood up in a chair and turned the radio on. The radio growled and reluctantly the station came in amid continuing static. Music came through the large speaker resting on the radio and clock shelf. The boy started turning the dial for something more interesting.

"Charles!" his mother demanded, "turn the radio back to the music station!"

Her look was almost as serious as her voice, so he turned the dial back on the old Atwater Kent metal-cased radio and watched her prepare dinner. Charles wanted to take the top off the radio to study the neatly painted electrical boxes and parts inside but knew he would need to wait for another day when the radio was off and his mother was not standing over him. The yellow-eyed beans had swelled and filled a large enamel pan of boiling water. His mother was adding molasses, brown sugar, spices, and salt pork to the watery beans. After stirring the mixture a few minutes, she put the lid on and turned the oil-flame down on the burner to let it simmer.

She went over to put her arm around his shoulder and lead him into the next room. The boy had fine features like her, but he was very small for his nine years and fragile-looking. She sat him down on the sofa asking him what he would like to do while dinner was cooking.

"Will you play a game of 'War' with me?" he asked with his face lit up.

"Sure," she answered. "Go get the cards. They're probably in your sister's room."

He returned with the cards and they began to play the matching game. As they played, he felt his mother's eyes on him. He would get excited as he carefully placed his cards in the stack when their cards had equal values. Then his face would fall when his overturned card was weaker than her top card.

2

"Charles, you take after my side of the family," his mother said as she studied him. "You'll not be a big person like your father. You'll have to rely on your wits to work and survive in a world where most men will be bigger and stronger than you. Sometimes strength is very important for work, like the man who brings the big block of ice for the ice chest every week. There are jobs and work that require mental instead of physical strength and for them you must be good in school and study hard." She looked at him intently, "Do you understand what I'm telling you?"

Charles nodded as he matched her jack and started piling cards on it. In his mind he had a picture of the iceman coming into the back porch with the big cube of ice between the calipers that held it against the black rubber square around his shoulders. Charles would wonder why the ice never slipped from the steel tongs when the man gripped only one handle instead of two. When he started the first grade in school he noticed that most of the boys were taller. Somehow, he expected to catch up with them but over the years he began to realize that he would always be smaller. He pushed his mother's statements out of his mind. It would be many years before he would be old enough to work and he could think about it then.

The storm suddenly shook the windows and Rose began worrying about June, who was at her piano lesson. The aroma of baked beans started to waft into the room and Charles noticed it with an acknowledging smile. "Can I have something to eat?" he asked.

"The beans won't be ready for a half-hour yet." She answered. "Don't go near the breadbox. Besides, you know we all eat dinner together."

The front door opened with a burst of sound, snow, and cold air. June was home. "Damn, it's miserable out there!" she exclaimed. "I thought spring was coming! When the groundhog sticks his nose out he's going to have it frozen off this year!" She threw her coat and boots off with more noise and walked through the house into the kitchen. Standing in front of the stove, she held her hands out to warm them up. Her body was cold and immobile, but her mind was working as fast as ever. Now her thoughts left her lessons, which she took just to please her mother, and flew to her latest boyfriend. 'Maybe I have two boyfriends,' she thought, 'if I only can keep the old one and the new one apart somehow.' It wasn't that she didn't like the old one, it was just that the new one was more exciting and had money from a job. The boys flocked to this girl on foot, by bus, and many kinds of old cars. She enjoyed the chase and was proficient at keeping a few boys in the background at all times. She noticed that the ends of her long brown hair were wet and went upstairs to her bedroom to comb and fuss over it.

Rose recovered from the interruption and did not fail to notice that June had not said a word about her piano lessons. 'All she thinks about is boys. Sixteen years old and all she thinks about are boys. Maybe I'm wasting my money on the lessons,' she thought.

The card game was getting monotonous. Charles would win a big stack of cards from her and she would win them back. There never was a decisive winner of this game because of the odds from the continual shuffle of the cards. Soon the beans would be ready and she could go back to her kitchen. But Charles was looking bored and she decided to give him some food for thought.

"Charles," she asked, "do you remember when we lived in the city?"

"No," he answered, wondering what she would talk about. She always started conversations by asking him about something he had never seen or done.

"Do you know when we lived in the city there were times when your father couldn't find any work and was too proud to ask for help? And the Depression made it impossible for people to pay him sometimes when he did have jobs." Her voice stiffened as she spoke of the hard times. The first ten years of marriage had been good because Tom had been such a capable and hard-working man. He had done everything he had promised to her. There was a car, a home, everything a young woman could wish for. Then the Crash came and, after a few years, all the work and money dried up as companies began to lay workers off and fail.

"I used to borrow money and even groceries from our friends who still had jobs." Those were terrible times. Tom was too proud to borrow money from anybody, even her family. He would refuse handouts from neighbors and friends who had work. There were times when she had to take money from people and never let him know about it or where it came from. She grinned and looked at the little boy in the eye.

"Once your father got a job driving a horse and wagon for the insane asylum in Danvers because it was the only work he could find.

4

He hated it because people would laugh when he said he worked for the madhouse. He kept the job for over a year until he was able to get a good machinist job in a company doing defense work."

"Gee, why were things so bad for everybody?" Charles asked, "Why were there suddenly no jobs or money? How could men like father be out of work?" It was inconceivable that anybody as capable as his father could be out of work. People called every night and weekend for him to fix things or make things run for them.

"I really don't know," she answered, She was getting anxious to get back to the kitchen now. It was time to check the boiling potatoes with a fork. Tom would never eat an evening meal without potatoes. "I think the bankers and rich people with money did it. All I know is there was a lot of speculation by the rich people and that the whole economy crashed. I only hope some of them had to suffer along with the hard-working people like us. Put the cards away. I've got a job for you in the kitchen." With that she left.

When he came in she gave him a bowl and a new package of margarine. Dutifully he got a large brassy spoon (that had lost its silverplate over the years) from the drawer and opened up the square waxed carton. He dropped the pound of white solid oil into the bowl and opened the little package of red dye that came with it. Charles stabbed the dye into the cube and energetically beat the cube into a mass of white, red, and orange color. Gradually the mass softened taking on the pale-yellow color of margarine. He hated the margarine which his mother put on everything from sandwiches to potatoes. Butter was on the list of goods, including a car, they had to do without. His mother said that it would be easier for father to get to work with a car now that gas rationing was over and cars were being produced for civilians again. His father had some money saved in the bank from working overtime for many years during the war. Mother also said that he would never buy anything on credit again, not even an automobile, because of the bankruptcies some of their friends underwent during the Depression because they owed money and had no jobs when their creditors demanded payment. They had lost everything they possessed, even their furniture and pots and pans, before it was over. And it was a disgrace not to be able to pay household bills.

The front door opened with a rush of storm noise announcing Tom's arrival. He left his overshoes, overcoat, gloves, and hard straw hat in the hallway and walked through the living room to the kitchen carrying his empty lunchbox. Although the furnace still had coal burning in it, the warmest place in the house was next to the nickel-plated cast iron stove with the small stained mica window in the oven. He headed there to warm away the redness of his nose and ears. Tom was a solidly-built person used to hard physical work. Although he worked with his hands and back, on this day he wore the dark blue serge suit that he changed at the job. What he wore to the job was always different from what he wore on the job. Even the poorest person was expected to dress well for work.

"I was mighty lucky to make it home on the bus tonight," he said, with his prominent Nova Scotian backwoods twang. "'Likely the roads will be shut down afore long. Them snow plows are out, but they can't get everything cleared 'less the snow stops long enough to let 'em get caught up. I reckon there's already a foot of new snow on the ground."

He took off his suit jacket and tie and went down into the cellar. The furnace grates ground through the house as he shook the ashes down. There was a scraping noise as a flat shovel slid under the coal pile and heaved fuel into the furnace. The cast-iron door clanged shut as he appeared in the kitchen again with a White Owl cigar clamped between his teeth. He gave the band to Charles who put it on his thumb and admired the owl picture.

"There's a clinker stuck a'tween the grates. It'll be spring a'fore I can shut the furnace down 'n clean it out. It's too fearful hot to mess with now," he stated to Rose.

June appeared from the front and began serving dinner with her mother. The news had started on the radio. The air was full of the Nuremberg War trials which were beginning. Tom's presence kept everybody quiet because they knew he wanted to relax and listen to the radio before he settled down. But the news often made him very angry. He spoke the inevitable statement they had all heard before.

"We'd no need of them blasted prolonged trials so's they can let 'em go free anyway! They best just line them criminals up against the wall the way the Russians do 'n shoot 'em!" Tom complained. He was bitter about the War because he had lost so many friends and relatives overseas. An uncle was lost in Halifax in the first war when two Liberty ammunition ships blew up in the harbor with the force of a nuclear explosion wiping the whole city off the map. The only good thing about the War, as far as he was concerned, was that it ended the Depression and put people back to work.

Tom's train of thought took him back to his childhood in Nova Scotia. He missed the relatives and people on the farm. 'Those were happy times,' he thought, as he remembered fishing in the bay and the big cornfield in the backyard. Sometimes he wondered if he had made a mistake leaving his people and happy times behind. On cold and windy nights, when he was alone with his memories, he would think of the dances that he went to with his brother, Ralph. There were many sweet young girls with giggles and pigtails who eagerly looked forward to dancing with Tom and his brother on Saturday nights. Tom remembered rushing to the dances with a lust for the girls and life that would not be quieted until he encountered Rose and the quicksand of the Depression.

Charles started on his food while watching his sister. She was eating in a hurry. 'She does everything in a hurry,' he thought. 'I wonder what it's like to be in high school and have so many things to do. I'm always looking for things to do. Life is boring. There is so much to learn but when you get big you get too busy. I'll never get grown up anyway because it's so many years away and I'll never live that long. I'll probably get run over by a car or die from something terrible. Or there will probably be another World War and I will be killed like some of the people that Mother and Father knew.' His mind wandered off to the incident that he caused last week.

He had been over by the main street wandering around, looking for something to do. A truck came down the street noisily splashing through the melting snow. He threw a snowball expecting it to bounce off the body unnoticed. But the snowball hit the driver's door with a loud whack, and the startled driver suddenly slammed on the brakes, sliding the truck into a snowbank on the side of the road. The driver jumped out and chased Charles for a block, cursing and swearing, until he finally turned around to go back and dig his truck out. Charles ran an extra block to escape and hid in a snowbank for a long time. Once his heart stopped pounding, he snuck home hoping that nobody had seen what had happened. 'That's the last time I'll ever throw snowballs at trucks or cars,' he thought.

The dinner table conversation had turned to the usual chatter about relatives and boyfriends as the news ended. Rossini's "William Tell Overture" announced the arrival of the Lone Ranger on the radio and Charles listened intently through the background noise. Everybody had finished eating when the serial ended as the Masked Man and Tonto rode into the sunset with the 'Hi, ho, Silver' finale on completion of their good deed for the night. Jack Benny and gravel-voiced Rochester started their evening dialogue.

"June," Charles asked, "can I help you with your stamp collection before you start on your homework?"

"Sure," she answered. "As long as you leave when I tell you. I have a shorthand exam coming up and need to study."

He readily agreed and headed up the stairs to her room. Recently he had seen the Gregg Shorthand textbook in her room and did not understand why or how anybody could ever understand the scribbles and scrolls of the business language. Her room was interesting and he liked it because it was full of nice things. There were dolls, books, clothes all over the place, the stamp folders, make-up stuff, interesting perfumy smells—like Mother's room—and a flowered bedspread instead of his dull blue one. There were even pretty curtains with pictures of a lady in pink and blue all over it except the lace at the bottoms. His room had no curtains. The femininity of the surroundings attracted him as much as the masculinity of his father's room. He lay on the soft bed for a while until the clatter of dishes died away downstairs and his sister appeared.

She smiled at her little brother. 'He's such a quiet boy,' she thought. 'There are never any stories of him getting into trouble at school. I imagine he will change and be more outgoing when he gets older and goes to trade school to follow in his father's footsteps.'

"How's school coming along these days?" she asked knowing that he was bored with it.

"School's dull," he replied. "We're reading the dumb Dick and Jane books and I can already read on my own. I've read the Hardy Boys Mysteries Mother gave me several times over. I've got to do arithmetic homework tonight. I hate division and multiplication." He knew he was careless and made too many mistakes.

June brought out her stamp collection books, and a cigar box of loose items not filed. She seemed to receive some kind of stamps every week in the mail from a far-off place. Tonight, was Australian night and she sorted out a group of small cellophane envelopes neatly folded over at the top. The canceled stamps could be clearly seen inside. This lot had arrived in the past week. Charles worked with her for an hour as she carefully matched the stamps with the pictures in one of her books. She really did all the work but he enjoyed watching as if it were his own collection. Finally, they were finished and she shooed him off so she could do her homework.

Reluctantly he went downstairs where he shared the kitchen table with his father's cigar smoke rising from behind an evening newspaper. He carefully laid out his arithmetic book, two well-chewed erasers less pencils, a little red pencil sharpener, a gum eraser punctured by black pencil stabbings, and some of the unbleached thin tan paper to work on. After much scribbling and erasing he finished. The paper now had holes from erasing. Somehow, he always got good grades in school but it was a chore. Looking up he saw his mother waiting to take him to bed.

After Charles made a trip to the bathroom, Rose led him to his little room. He went directly to the corner table where a cup of clear liquid held a string suspended from a Popsicle stick. No sugar crystals had formed yet from his project to dissolve a vast amount of sugar in hot water and redeposit it as large crystals on the string. 'Maybe I need more time to make the rock candy,' he thought as he tugged at the bare string. He changed into his flannel pajamas and she kissed him goodnight.

"Say your prayers before you get in bed," she directed as she stood in the doorway.

Charles looked at her and kneeled down at the edge of his bed saying, "Now I lay me down to sleep. I pray the Lord my soul to keep. If I should die before I wake, I pray the Lord my soul to take." With that he jumped into bed. His mother was still in the doorway.

"Go to sleep now or the Sandman will come and get you!" she admonished and left the room.

Charles always had trouble sleeping at night. Ordinarily he would review the events of the day and the plans for tomorrow. Tonight, he was occupied by the noise of the storm. Tomorrow would be a great day. There had been no announcement about school closings on the radio tonight so the news would be saved for the early morning. He loved the cleanness of a new snowfall with the whole world blanketed in the sound-absorbing whiteness. Everything would be fresh and new when he woke up.

The noise of furnace grates grinding rose up to his room. His father was shaking and stoking the furnace for the night. Soon everybody would be in bed and the house would be quiet. That was the time Charles did not like. There was nothing to listen to. The stillness left him alone with his thoughts. 'I wonder what the Sandman would look like,' he thought. He didn't believe there really was such an entity to throw sand in his eyes to make him sleep. It was easy to believe in ghosts though and maybe there was a sandman ghost. Parents were always saying dumb things to scare him. Sometimes they disguised things so he would be confused and frightened without telling him what was really happening. They had a habit of giving him half answers to his questions. Maybe they didn't believe he would understand what they were talking about. Especially when he asked about the World War. Someday he would find out for himself. There must be some books he could find about it. He was already starting to read different things in the Lincoln Library encyclopedia that Mother had bought for June.

The wind and cold from the storm made him feel cold. He shivered and pulled the blankets and quilt over his head, drifting off to sleep.

Awhile later Rose suddenly woke up. Something was wrong. She rose and stood in her doorway. Rubbing the sleep from her eyes she saw Charles open the door of his room. He headed for the bathroom. Slowly he walked along the hallway where the stairs came up next to the bathroom. He followed the railing and as he reached the stair-break he started falling down the stairwell. She lunged for him and caught him just in time. With her arm around his waist she led him to the bathroom and back to his room. Not once did he say a word or open his eyes. He was still asleep.

During the night Charles had a dream in which he needed to go to the bathroom. In the dream he met his mother in the hallway. Then the dream faded away.

Chapter Two

A Day at School

*I*n the early morning darkness Charles woke to the grinding sound of his father shaking down the furnace. The noise continued for a few minutes vibrating its way up the open radiators of the house. Then it was silent and Charles fell asleep again. He dreamed that he was a speck of dust in the universe of events. He was helpless and watched as people and things moved around him, a stranger in a universe of things larger and more complicated than his comprehension. Like a visitor to earth, he was an observer rather than a participant in the circus that is life. He could not reach out and touch anything in the dream. At last he fell off into a deep sleep and the dream left him.

When he woke the first thing he noticed was his cold feet. His blankets were pulled up and his feet were sticking out the bottom. He looked up at the window and could see only the icy frost coating the inside. A second later he was rubbing the frosting away from the center of the pane with the palm of his hand.

"Wow!" he said when he saw the great plain of snow reaching away to the house across the street. The storm had ended. He put his slippers on and dashed down to the kitchen.

"Is there any school today?" he asked anxiously.

His mother was about to come up and wake him for school. The radio was on and the school closing announcements would begin shortly but she wanted him ready in case he had to go.

"I'll let you know when I hear something. Meanwhile you'd better get dressed and brush your teeth." She watched him go from the room as she put away the large round cardboard box of Quaker Oats that Tom had used for breakfast. He would salt two cups of

12

boiling water and add the large flakes until they swelled up like a large gelatin sponge. Then he would put it in a large bowl with milk and sugar. That, toast and tea were his whole breakfast. She turned the box around on the shelf so that the Quaker on the box smiled outward at her.

Charles locked himself in the bathroom and poured the pumice and peppermint white Lyons toothpowder from the tin can into his palm. He wet the brush and dipped it into the powder until it stuck. When he finished brushing he explored the medicine cabinet. There was still some Farmer John's cod-liver oil in the thin tall bottle with the rounded shoulders. He used to take the oily stuff by the tablespoonful whenever his mother thought he had a cold. "Yuck!" he said out loud as he stuck his tongue out at the thought of the dosage. The next discovery was a round tin can of Doan's Little Liver Pills. A stuck top was finally twisted off spilling some of the hard pea-sized pills on the linoleum. He picked them up in a hurry so nobody could discover what he was up to. His curiosity was aroused. He examined Tom's dark brown leather strop worn thin in places by the razor being slapped against it. A shaving mug still showed traces of dried soap on the rim with a boar-bristle brush stuck inside. He gingerly opened the pearl-handled razor part way and quickly closed it. Next, he unscrewed a large jar of Vaseline and worked a dab into his hair to hold it down, then combed it until it was shiny and flat. Kitchen noises caught his attention and he rushed downstairs to join his sister and mother.

When he arrived at the kitchen his mother put out his creamed wheat porridge. He poured milk into it to make the steam go away. As it cooled off he brought up his latest discovery.

"What are the Doan's Little Liver pills for, Mother?"

She gave him a funny look meaning it was none of his business and stated:

"They are for women and I don't need to tell you why."

With that she had left him with another mystery to solve. Maybe one of the kids down the street would know, he thought as he added sugar to his breakfast.

The radio started announcing school closings as June rushed into the room to get her breakfast. She looked at the table and realized that she had a choice of whole wheat or cream of wheat porridge.

"Ugh!" she exclaimed. "Why can't we have something decent for breakfast like other people!"

"Quiet, Sis, I'm trying to listen to the radio!" Charles yelled, afraid to miss the good news on the radio as the announcer read off his list of streets closed for plowing and the few schools and agencies not open for business as usual. The school closings suddenly concluded and Charles realized that he did not have the day off after all.

He went out the front door and brought the milk bottles in with their wire basket. Carefully he examined the bottles for ice in the necks and could see none. Darn, he thought, it isn't even cold enough to freeze the milk. Maybe the milkman was late today. During the winter it was usually cold enough to freeze the milk and the degree of coldness was determined by the amount of ice in the milk bottles. He loved to see a thick plug of ice in the neck between the milk and the cream. No ice meant that the snow would thaw quickly and that winter was coming to an end.

His mother took the milk and finished dressing him for the cold trip to school. Handed his lunch pail and books, he stepped out into the cold. The wind had died down. There was a wonderful silence and cleanness about the front yard and street. He stood still a minute testing the depth of the snow by looking at the depth of his father's booted footsteps leading out to the street which had narrow trails of tire tracks going to the plowed main street. The snow was more than a foot deep in places. Charles went over to the lawn bush and shook the snow off it. Then he walked until he was at the house next door.

He beat on the door with small mittened fists until a young blonde woman opened it. "Come in, Charles. Mary Anne will be ready in a minute." She left him standing in the hallway so he would not track snow into the rest of the house. A minute later a small slender blonde girl with a ponytail hanging down from a red woolen cap came through the door.

"Hello, Charles," she said with a smile. She saw the gleam in his eyes and shared it because today would be an exciting walk to school in the new snow.

"Hi, Mary Anne," he said, also smiling and very glad to see her. He always looked forward to walking to school with her in the morning. She would chatter about little girl interests like her dolls, things that her little sister had done, and what her mother had

14

gossiped over the dinner table. He would share things with her and together they would hike the mile to school along the main street. All the schoolchildren had to get to school by a ride from parents or in small groups on their own. Getting home was different because they would be marched back in a large group by an older boy from the fifth grade. Charles especially liked the walk with Mary Anne because it was a half-hour of freedom from the supervision of adults.

After walking along for five minutes, chattering and kicking the powdered snow, they came to the place where they sometimes saw the spy. He was not there this morning. Mary Anne expressed her disappointment by stating that he probably was afraid to come out in the snow.

"Maybe it doesn't snow in Germany," she said with a snicker.

"Sure, it does," Charles declared. He had seen snow in a war movie about the War in Europe. He knew the War was over, but this man definitely looked like a spy and someday he would be caught and shot. His father would see to it because he hated spies and war criminals. They passed by the bus stop knowing they would see him again.

They walked past the big hill with the waterfall. The water was coursing through the snow, disappearing in places. It left a dark channel through the whiteness of the trees and ground. They knew better than to stop and play because there was just enough time to get to school with the snow slowing them down.

Small groups and individual children were walking the same direction down the sides of the main street which had been plowed, leaving a temporary wave of snow along the sides. There were no snowball fights because the snow was too dry and powdery. In time there would, as always, be. It was impossible to mix these children and snow without getting a snow fight. The chemistry for a duel would be there later on when the snow softened.

The hill sloped into a gentle field and at the end of the field, across the street where some houses were sparsely scattered, a square wooden building stood next to the street. This was the goal of all the children. Charles and Mary Anne arrived and after shedding their overshoes and leggings they were in the classroom where again they were together. They were the same age. He sat in front of her near the rear of the classroom which was their home away from home for most of the year.

The teacher was a trim woman in her late 30's. She had been wearing a hairnet over her brown hair lately since she found silver strands of greying hair when she combed it out one day not long ago. The hairnet made her look older than the premature grey hairs would. She was a single woman with plain features, a broad Danish brow and high cheekbones that attracted the wrong kind of man to her. Her parents had sent her to the State Teachers College when she finished high school twenty years earlier, that being the only school her parents could afford. The state attended to its own needs by providing free education for the people who would serve it in limited functions in the future. Many young women of above average intelligence pursued teaching because it provided a professional means of self-support in case they did not find proper husbands.

She surveyed the room full of small children. They would chatter away until she called the room to order. 'Let them socialize a minute longer,' she thought. 'They can unwind now so I can have their attention when I need it.' She had no children of her own but here she had twenty. She loved to teach and listen to them. 'Most people have only a few children, but I am better off because I have many,' she thought. 'I don't have to change their diapers when they are babies or wash and iron their clothes. Mine is the best part though, teaching them some fundamentals so they will have a decent start in life. There are smarter and stricter teachers than I, but I like my children and I know I do a good job. The salary is small, but people show me some respect when they find out I am a teacher.' The clock struck eight and she called her children to order.

When the drone of whispering and books being shuffled died down the morning routine started with a salute to the American flag. After the children finished reciting, Miss Pritchett had them sing the national anthem. The children's voices filled the room as they got in tune with each other. Miss Pritchett smiled as she sang. She always loved to hear her children sing. It sounded beautiful and helped settle the class down for a day's work. When they finished she seated them and got out her Bible. She read the Lord's Prayer to them taking time to go over each word slowly so they would hear clearly even if they didn't understand everything.

When she finished, there was a moment of silence. Then she asked Mary Anne what the prayer meant. She liked Mary Anne very much. She was her favorite child this year. Mary Anne was not especially intelligent, but she was warm and outgoing. She would always innocently and fearlessly answer any question honestly and simply without getting easily misled and confused like some of the children. She was a very pretty child radiating a glowing disposition Miss Pritchett remembered from her own childhood.

"The prayer," Mary Anne stated firmly, "means that we are children of God." She remembered hearing the same phrase at Sunday School more than once. She smiled knowing that she had given a good answer to the question and that the teacher liked her.

Miss Pritchett thanked her and looked around the room. The children wanted more. 'Perhaps she could get a debate started to let her children think a bit more about the subject. Religion was a part of all their lives. It was a guide to doing good. Without it there would be more hate and evil in the world.' Her mind wandered back to the classroom. She asked Charles to tell what he thought about the Lord's Prayer. Charles was always good for a debate because he had keen insight into how things worked. He also had a great curiosity. On other occasions however, he would be completely off base because he was a daydreamer and not concentrating on the subject.

Charles looked at her blankly trying to think of what to say. He was terrible at remembering things that came easily to Mary Anne or most of the other children. He looked around and got mixed grins and stares from some of the boys in the class.

"The Lord's Prayer is a story to let us know that if bad things happen to us and we die we will go to heaven." With that he sat down and waited for the teacher's response. Charles didn't think he gave a good answer. Religion always bothered him. In Sunday School the teacher always talked about sins and the Bible. People were always killing people or being killed and going to Heaven or Hell. One of the kids down the street had said that there was another place called Purgatory. It was an in-between place where bad people stayed when God had trouble making up his mind which place to send them to. I suppose it's like needing to go to the bathroom and they won't let you get there, he thought. There couldn't be anything more terrible.

Miss Pritchett thanked him and started pacing across the front of the room to get their attention.

"Children, when you grow up you will be expected to do things that will be very hard. Some of you in this class will become mothers and fathers to raise children. Others will have jobs and work hard to make a living. Sooner or later in life there will be an opportunity to steal or hurt someone else. I want you to be good children and good people when you grow up. As the Bible says, do unto others as you would have them do unto you. Think of all the murders that are committed in the world and the wars that kill innocent people. If you want to go to Heaven when you die you must be a good person to get there. The Lord's Prayer says that He will help you get to Heaven but only if you are good." Then she told them to be silent for a minute and think of someone they knew who had died and gone to Heaven.

Later that afternoon, after a lunch of peanut butter and jelly sandwiches wrapped in waxed paper and milk provided by the school in small bottles, Charles looked out the window and saw the sun beating down on the snow-covered field across the street. He knew the sun would heat the snow enough to soften it so it would make good compact snowballs. The class was reading the Dick and Jane books slowly out loud. Charles was bored because the story was nonsense and he had read the book during the first week of school. He looked up at the clock. The time was 2:45. He had an idea. If the clock had a hundred minutes it would be easier to tell time than always having to calculate from sixty minutes. Maybe ten hours would be easier too because then he wouldn't have to know the a.m. from the p.m. Telling time was dumb because nothing added up easily. The math problems of hours and minutes were tedious and he was always making mistakes. He imagined a clock with one hundred minutes on it. The fifteen-minute quarter-hour would be a twenty-five-minute quarter just like money. A silver quarter would be twenty-five cents. Thus, the half-hour would be fifty minutes instead of thirty and so on.

The class stopped reading out loud and was instructed to read by themselves. Charles turned around and whispered to Mary Anne.

"Wouldn't it be a great idea if the clock had a hundred minutes instead of sixty?" Mary Anne looked perplexed. She had no idea what he was talking about.

"Quiet, the teacher is watching us," she said as Miss Pritchett noticed the sounds in the back of the room.

Miss Pritchett's method to cure disturbance was to expose the perpetrator, not ignore him. Accordingly, she asked Charles to stand up and tell the class what he had said to Mary Anne. If it was good enough for her it was good enough for the class to hear.

Charles stood up and blushed. The other children watched him, snickering and giggling, always pleased to have a break from their lessons. Charles stammered, then told the class that if a clock had one hundred minutes instead of sixty it would be easier to tell time.

The teacher looked at him in surprise. A hundred-minute clock would be absurd. Clocks had sixty minutes and it had always been that way.

"Children," she said, "clocks have sixty minutes because that is the correct way to tell time. A hundred-minute clock would be nonsense. It would be metric, based on multiples of the number ten, which is the European system of measurement. We are not concerned with these things here. Charles, go stand in the corner for disturbing the class. I'll tell you when you can return to your seat." With that she returned to the work at her desk while the class resumed reading.

Charles, embarrassed and flushed, stood in the corner of the room until he was recalled. He was careful not to say any more until the bell rang for the end of the school day.

As they were being herded home by the fifth-grader, Mary Anne scolded him.

"You say the dumbest things, Charles," she admonished. Charles said nothing in defense. He needed to learn to keep his mouth shut.

The hundred-minute clock idea kept running through Charles' head, however. 'Maybe nobody would listen to him and maybe the whole world would have to change to 100 minutes, which would be too hard to do. Perhaps there was a 100-minute clock in Europe someplace where things were done in hundreds or thousands.' Suddenly he got an idea. 'What if he, Charles, had a hundred-minute clock that only he used. He could use sixty minutes to deal with the people and things around him as they are on a sixty-minute hour. And he could use the other forty minutes for his private time to daydream or think about things. It would be a special and exclusive time for himself.'

As soon as he got home, he changed his clothes and went out to play. His first stop was Harry's place several houses down the street. Harry was busy doing his chores and Charles had to wait for him. He lived in a big house that had a large garage with a loft in it. His family

19

was rich because his father was a lawyer and his mother worked as a secretary. Harry had a list of chores to do each day because his parents were not home to do them. They were little things like taking the trash out, shovel snow, feed the cat, etc. He was also two years older than Charles and much taller. That gave him leadership status with the kids on the street who were either younger or smaller. His leadership was also of a natural quality because he was not overbearing or possessive. He was just a nice kid to be around. Besides one could have fun with him and learn things because his family had a car and he had a big Lionel electric train set in his room.

Harry finally got free and they went to his room to plan the afternoon. He was a planner. Everything had to be planned in advance. It was the way his family operated. Harry's sister would go to college in a few years like her parents, and he was expected to follow. There was a family plan for everything and the members of the family were expected to coordinate everything to the central plan. This contrasted with Charles' family where everybody would be left to their own fate when they grew up. Harry's family was goal oriented; Charles' was subject to the worldly environment.

"What are we doing today?" Harry asked as they settled down.

"I want to build a snow fort." Charles responded. "My mother said that the snow will not last long and there probably won't be another snowfall until next winter." Charles had never built a real snow fort. He had started one in his yard once but had not made much progress before he gave up from the cold and early darkness. He had worked on it for a whole week after school and was very disappointed in the results. He had seen a terrific one that the Baker Street gang on the next street had made. It was almost as high as he was tall and had very thick walls. Every kid on the street had worked on it and when they finished they hardened the structure by spraying water on it late in the day so it would freeze.

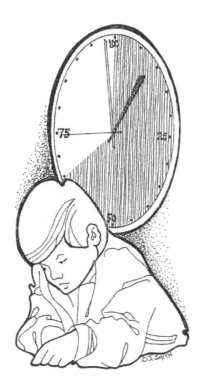

The magnificent fort lasted over a month before a warm spell melted it down after slowly shrinking it for a week.

There was a tall fence that went down the backyard of Charles' house to the end of the street. It effectively divided the children on the streets. The children on Charles' street all grouped together in an informal gang led by Harry. They were known as the Marsh Street gang. The street was named Marsh Street because it led into the great marsh. Children on the next street over were grouped into another gang led by a big dumb kid named Jack. They were known as the Baker Street gang. Relations between the separate gangs were generally friendly. The gangs were family-oriented and bound by neighborhood rather than conflict with other groups.

Harry thought about the suggestion for a minute. It would be nice to have a fort before the warm weather arrived. The new snow was already softening and would soon pack very easily. The only problem was that there would not be much time to build it.

"If we can get some help to build it in a couple of days it would be a good idea," he said. "Let's see if the other kids can do it with us."

They left and started making the rounds of the street to see who was available. Only two of the kids were free. One was Adam, a nervous feisty kid whose parents were always fighting. The other was Richard, who was very chubby. His mother was always baking things. She was also fat. Whenever Charles came near her house he could smell the good things baking in the oven. She was the only person on the street who still baked her own bread. A discussion started on the snow fort. Adam said that he was tired of the snow and cold and was not interested in doing any more with it. Richard said that he was interested in the project but his mother told him to stay home. That meant they had to build it at his house if they wanted to do it at all. Richard's backyard was very small so that was out. He went into the house to get permission from his mother to build it in the front of the house. His mother strongly said no. The fort project was dead.

The boys milled around the front of the house for a while getting bored and cold. Adam threw a snowball at the shed in the back of the house. Everybody followed and, in a few minutes, they were trying to see who could get closest to the handles in the middle where the doors joined. The shed was plastered with spots of snow where the snowballs had compressed themselves to the boards. The snowballs made a loud whacking noise as they hit the loose doors of the shed. The kids started yelling and getting excited at the new game.

Suddenly Richard's mother burst out of the house and screamed at them, "Get out of here you hellions, all of you! Go play somewhere else! Stop making all that noise! Come in, Richard, I have something better for you to do than drive me crazy!" She stood on the back porch with her face red from exertion.

Richard retreated into his house. Gradually the group broke up. The fun for this afternoon was ruined. Charles followed Harry to his house. They played with his train set for the rest of the afternoon until it was time to go home for dinner.

When Charles got home his sister was practicing on the piano. The old upright player piano was a bit out of tune. So was his sister. June's heart was not in it. Her mother insisted that she practice at least every other day and get private lessons once a week to improve. June had just arrived home from school. School had been out for several hours while she stood outside the schoolhouse talking to the boys until time ran out and she was frozen stiff. She finished the piece and looked at Charles. Her concentration dissolved.

"Play a roll on the player for me?" Charles asked. He always had to ask someone else to do it for him. His legs were not long enough to reach the pedals. Rose probably would not let him play even if he could.

"O.K., little brother," June answered, anxious to do something other than reading sheet music. She opened up the wing doors in the front of the piano and went into a cabinet to take out a long cardboard box. Then she took the roll of perforated paper out of the box and fit it over the shiny steel drum with slots cut in it. The piano doors were left open so Charles could see the paper roll over the drum. Finally, she sat down and began pedaling. The keys began to magically move down as if invisible fingers pressed on them. Charles watched with fascination. He was not interested in the music, just the mechanics of producing it. His sister had told him once that the pedals created a vacuum that made air come in the holes in the paper and that made the keys work. He didn't understand but he always enjoyed watching and listening.

It was starting to get dark out. Charles wandered around the house looking for something to do after his sister had disappeared into the sanctity of her room. Thinking about the next day Charles bumped into his mother. "Mother, can I take a can of fat to the store tomorrow?" he asked. She would save up cans of excess fat from her cooking and let him take them to the store for a dime each. The fat would be reprocessed somewhere and made into soap.

"I'm sorry, Charles. The store won't buy the fat anymore. Now the War is over they don't need it for the War Effort. I'll have to throw it out from now on." She looked sadly at him. He had a whole box of dimes she had let him keep from his trips to the store. That was his savings bank.

Charles looked at his mother and did not say anything. He was disappointed. Now that the War was over, everything was changing. He would need to find other ways to earn money. They stopped using ration stamps and coupons some time ago. He had some of the little red pressed cardboard ration currency hidden away with his collection of miscellaneous things, like a broken watch that someone had given him and a music box machine without the music box.

He went into the living room and turned on a small lamp with a colorful painted shade of Niagara Falls on it. When the lightbulb inside heated up, a small round piece of tin with slots in it slowly moved around the outside of the lightbulb. This gave a shadowy effect to the light reaching the shade and made the water on the shade appear to be in motion. Charles watched the lamp for a while until it was time for dinner.

After dinner the phone rang and June was on it for an hour discussing her innermost feelings about boys with a girlfriend. Charles was working a jigsaw puzzle near her in the living room. The sawmill picture was difficult and thus boring to work on. 'Almost as boring as Sis' telephone conversation,' Charles thought.

Rose entered the living room loudly stating her annoyance about June's preoccupation with boys and having a monopoly on the telephone.

"June, if you don't get off that phone in one minute, I'll have your father speak to you."

June hesitated, then informed her friend that she had run out of time. She hung up the phone. She was her father's pet but she did not want to incur his wrath after a hard day at work. He was gone twelve hours each day between taking buses and overtime on the job. When he got home he was always tired and hungry as a bear. But he liked hard work and now the Depression was over, there was plenty of work to be had. A moment later the phone rang. June answered thinking it was a boyfriend. It was someone wanting to know if Tom could fix their oil stove. The burners kept going out. She got her father.

Ten minutes later he left to catch a bus to the customer's house. With his metal toolbox in hand, he did not utter a word of complaint. It was very cold and dark out but he would take any extra work he could. He had not yet recovered from the emptiness and poverty of the Depression when there was never enough work or money. His family saw very little of him except on weekends. That was the price he paid to support them. He was a man hardened by the Depression.

Later that night as Charles laid in bed he contemplated what it would be like to be a man. 'I don't want to work as hard as my father,' he thought. 'I want to do all the things that big people are supposed to do, but I don't want to become a working slave. Why must life be so harsh with wars and people working all the time? It would be nice to marry when I grow up and to have children of my own. I'll marry Mary Anne. He smiled to himself. I like her a lot.'

A picture of the metric clock appeared again. I will take my forty minutes now, Charles thought. I will take it and think of the day when I take a trip on a big train, like the express in the movies. The long hand of the clock moved up to eighty and then ninety minutes as Charles rode a great noisy, smoking train with huge wheels to sleep.

Chapter Three

The Spy

They were walking to school when Mary Anne saw the spy.

"There he is!" she exclaimed. The snow had turned to slush and they had been walking along a narrow path created by the footsteps of schoolchildren and people who walked to the bus stop. Every day they watched for the spy on the way to school but he was only occasionally waiting for a bus when they went by. She clutched Charles' hand and stopped abruptly.

Charles stopped with her. His heart started pounding. He looked around for the other kids from the street and saw nobody. Today they had all gone ahead. Charles didn't know if they had seen the spy. They probably hadn't, he reasoned, because they would have run back to his house to tell him.

The spy was dressed in his usual suspicious attire. He wore a grey round Homburg hat with a black silk band around the bottom edge, black leather gloves, and a grey overcoat with a black felt collar to match. Then there were the shiny black leather boots with his trousers bloused inside the tops, not like the galoshes or rubbers that most people wore. He was a thin man in his 50's. A bony rib of a nose protruded from his face. They had always seen him carrying a worn black leather briefcase in one hand and a tightly bound black umbrella in the other. The umbrella probably had a needle-sharp sword inside and God knew what he carried in the briefcase. He always stood tall and erect while waiting for the bus. There was a definite military air about him. His face had a coarse cruel and hardened European look. He had to be a foreigner. If he had spoken

26

to the children they knew to expect a foreign accent, probably German or Prussian, but he had not.

Charles stood breathless. 'What if the spy saw them and knew that they knew,' he thought.

"Mary Anne," he whispered, "let's cut across the lawn behind him so he doesn't see us." She gave Charles a nod and they both ran around the lawn of the nearby house and circled around him. Afterward they looked back to see if he was still there.

"Did he see us?" Mary Anne asked as she looked back partly out of breath.

"No," Charles answered. "We must have a meeting with the kids on the street to see where he lives and find out what he's doing here," Charles answered, taking control of the situation.

"I don't want any part of it," Mary Anne stated. "He scares me. I don't want to get kidnapped or murdered by a spy."

They arrived at school and the matter was forgotten until they were released to be marched home in the usual gaggle. Since the group was organized by classroom, Charles did not see the other kids from his street until he got home and changed.

Charles told Harry what he saw and they went up and down the street rounding up the rest of the gang. They collected in the loft over Harry's garage to discuss the emergency. It was cold and dark. A small amount of light radiated into the empty garage below from windows on each side of the building. Harry lit a candle. The children's breathing made tiny clouds of steam. The candle helped light up the room but there was no help for the cold. It would be a short meeting.

All of the gang was there. This was the first time in months they had been together at the same time. Adam, Richard, Harry, Charles, and Merle were all present. Richard was the new kid on the block. His family had moved in at year-end from the City. He was big for his age and quite outgoing. He was anxious to be included in the gang's activities and had heard all about the spy. Merle had a dark complexion. June had told Charles she heard he was a full-blooded Indian from someplace in Northern Canada. He was very quiet and usually spoke only when spoken to.

Harry opened the discussion:

"Charles and Mary Anne saw the spy today at the bus stop on the way to school. Did anybody else see him?" There was no response. "What are we going to do about the spy?" he asked.

"Gosh, let's tell the police about him," Adam volunteered.

"How can we tell the police if we don't know anything about him?" Ralph scoffed. "We don't even know where he lives or has any secret radios or guns."

"How do you know he really is a spy?" Merle asked. He was always the skeptic.

Charles got all excited and told everybody what the spy looked like and that he knew he had to be a spy. "All we have to do is to get some proof or evidence," he concluded.

"Why don't we wait for him to return home and follow him to where he lives?" Harry suggested. "We can take turns waiting in the bushes near the bus stop until he comes back. Then we can follow him to his house and find out what he's up to."

"That's a great idea," Merle exclaimed. "We can double up with two kids for an hour each shift. Then one of us can follow him while the other kid goes back to get the rest of the gang."

Adam suggested that he go home and get a bag of small coal lumps from his cellar so the one who was following the spy could leave a trail until the other kids caught up.

"That's a swell idea, Adam," Harry declared. "Go home and get the coal. First let's toss coins to see who the odd and even partners are."

They tossed coins with Adam and Richard tails, Merle and Charles heads. Harry volunteered to stay behind to be the Commander and maintain the headquarters in his house where there was a clock to tell time since there were no watches among the children. Harry knew where it was nice and warm for a proper commander of the troops. Adam went home and came running back in a few minutes with a large bag of coal.

"It's getting cold out there," Adam stated as he climbed up the stairs into the loft. "Let's make the shifts half an hour each or we'll get frozen to death." The new schedule was readily agreed to and Charles went off with Merle and the bag of coal to the designated hiding place. The other three children went into Harry's house where it was warm. Harry started his chores while the other children watched the clock and discussed what they knew about spies from the war movies they had seen.

Charles and Merle trudged along the main street until they came to a big hedge in front of a house. They hid behind the hedge hoping nobody would see them.

"Could the spy have already gone home?" Merle asked, not looking forward to the cold vigil.

"I doubt it," Charles answered. "Nobody ever comes home before dark." He knew that only schoolchildren, babies, and mothers were home during the day. It would be unheard of for anybody else to arrive early unless they got sick or hurt. His mother had let him stay home once when he had pneumonia and the teacher sent him home on another day with a bad cold. Big people rarely stayed home because they did not get paid when they missed work.

It was late in the afternoon and a great relief to the cold children when Adam and Richard arrived to relieve them of their duty. The hedge was such a good barrier that Adam and Richard did not see Charles and Merle until they stood up and waved. While walking back Charles felt the cold in his fingers and toes. He complained to Merle that the next shift would be harder. "I don't mind the cold," Merle said. He was sincere. He had felt the cold at first but as time wore on he had gotten used to it. The cold had not gone away; he had just conditioned himself to bear it. He had been taught by his parents never to complain unless he really had to. Complaining would not change things, they said. Only he and God could change things.

At Harry's house they drank hot chocolate and continued the discussions about spies and things in general. Later on it was their shift again as darkness settled in around them. The spy did not come home. Every fifteen minutes a bus stopped and they watched everybody but the spy disembark. Finally Charles saw his father get off the bus. He stayed hidden in the bushes as he saw his father go home. Charles suppressed the desire to yell to his father and let him know where he was but he did not want to expose the position. A few minutes later the next shift arrived. Charles informed Harry it was time to go home because his father was there and dinner would be ready. If he did not get home his sister would be sent to look for him and he would be in trouble. Harry agreed and the boys left. That evening Charles called Harry to find out if the final shift had located the spy. They had not. They would have to postpone to a future day catching their mysterious agent.

Chapter Four

The Contest

Charles passed a row of trash cans on the way to school. On trash day people hauled the barrels of ashes up from their cellars and lined them up next to the curb. All the trash was burned in the furnaces with the coal for heat. Flattened tin cans and bottles lay on top the ashes. Newspapers were also piled on top, some tied in neat bundles, others anchored with tin cans or other metal scraps. The items on top of the ashes were then segregated by the trash men and recycled for the War conservation effort. Soon the official conservation effort would cease and the trash men, in collusion with the dump pickers, would engage in their own recycling enterprises.

The melting snow had turned the countryside into mud and water. Before the last of it was gone, blades of grass were poking up through with renewed vigor and life. The atmosphere was fresh with a new warmth. Buds were swelling and breaking out of the branches of the elm and maple trees. A change was in the air.

Charles was back to wearing knickers again, instead of leggings. He hated them and begged his mother to let him wear the long trousers the older kids were wearing. She declined. "There's nothing wrong with knickers," she had said. Rose was always the last person in the world to change anything. She also made him wear suspenders instead of a belt. Worn metal snaps were always wearing out and he found himself bunching more and more of the waistband into the claws to make them hold. Worse yet, he would now be changing into short pants after school. Charles was also tired of his blue winter coat. The elastic was frayed and dirty at the collar and wrists. He would be glad to discard it as soon as the cool mornings warmed up.

Charles took a worn tin tube of Chapstick out of his pocket and threw it in the street. He would not need it with the warmer weather. His cracked and bleeding lips had healed. Winter was over. Today was Friday. It was time to plan the weekend.

"What are you doing tomorrow?" he asked Mary Anne.

"Oh, we're visiting relatives in New Hampshire tomorrow." She answered, knowing she would rather be home or playing with some of the girls on the street.

"Mother said as soon as the weather cleared up we must visit her family. We haven't seen them for a long time. My grandmother has a big farm with cows and chickens. Sometimes it's fun going there." Mary Anne liked the farm but hated to sit around being quiet and polite while the old people talked about politics and other people.

"Besides," she added, "my father just got new tires for his Ford and now we can go places."

Charles had not made any plans for the weekend outside the usual Saturday afternoon movie which he always looked forward to. This Saturday one of the double feature films was the Walt Disney animation, "Bambi." Charles had heard it was a very good movie, so good he would have to go early to get a place in the line before it sold out. The theatre was always busy on Saturdays. He hated some of the movies that played there, such as the romance films, dumb dancing musicals, or complicated murder mystery movies. He liked the cartoons but what he liked best of all were the war movies and the Movietone War News shown between the features. This past year he missed the Pacific Theater and Western Front war news on the news clips since the war ended. Charles did not know it yet but the school and his father had some plans for his weekend.

At school Miss Pritchett was preparing for the final fund-raising event of the year. It was spring flower time. She handed out colored brochures with flower pictures to each of the children.

"Children," she said authoritatively, "Every spring we must ask you to help your school raise money for supplies. As you know, there is never enough money to buy everything the teachers need for their classroom. I'd like you to take the brochures home and show them to your family, friends, and neighbors. I want you to ask them to buy the packages of flower seeds for ten cents each to help your school. I expect you to make a serious attempt to sell as many as you can. There is a prize for the child who sells the most seeds. Be sure to keep a list of the people who buy so you can get the flower seeds to the right people when they arrive. I want to see your orders and the money on Friday next week. That will give you a week to contact everybody that you know. Now turn to the back of the colored brochure." With that there was a rustle of paper as the children turned the colorful pages over. "Use this page to list the orders. This list must be turned in with the money next week. Write your name at the top of the list right now before you forget."

She started talking about how nice the flowers were and how easy they were to sell by showing the colored brochure to people. Last year the flower campaign had been very successful and she had received almost $100 for her classroom supplies. Half of the sales were profit, as the seeds cost five cents per package. Since it was extra unbudgeted money, each classroom got to use all the profits it generated for a party or prizes for the spelling bees.

Charles looked at the brochure. Some of the names were hard to pronounce so he would just show the pictures to people and copy the names down. He wanted to win the prize very badly. He didn't remember what the prizes were the last year but he knew that it would be something special. This would give him something to do over the weekend. He looked forward to the contest.

"The flower seeds will be delivered to you about a week after you turn the money and the list in," the teacher was concluding, "Remember now it's very important to do a good job selling them. They're beautiful flowers and we'll all benefit from the proceeds." With that she dismissed the class for the weekend.

That evening Charles sold a package each to his mother and father. It would be easy to sell the flowers to everybody and win the prize. Nobody could work as hard as he would.

The next morning Rose informed Charles he needed to get his hair cut before he went to the movies. She also informed him he would be helping his father put the garden in after church on Sunday. The barbershop was in the town square near the theatre. Charles hated to get his hair cut. There was always a wait and the old man would clip and buzz the hair off that took so long to grow. He did not like the barbershop at all. Besides, it would take away from his seed-selling time.

Saturday morning Charles went up and down the street knocking on doors to sell his flowers. Many of the neighbors had kids in the same school so he avoided these places. When he came home several hours later he had sold only ten packages. He recorded the sales on the brochure but didn't bother to keep a separate list for himself. He would remember the orders when the flowers came in.

His mother gave him fifty cents. A quarter was for the barber. The remaining quarter would give him fifteen cents for the movie, a nickel for a candy bar, and a nickel for the bus ride home because it was usually dark by then. He usually would avoid the bus ride even though it was a two-mile walk, so he could buy two candy bars or ten cent popcorn. The only time he ever took a bus was in the winter when it was cold and dark. Even then he had succumbed to temptation several times this past winter and arrived home with ears, toes, nose and fingers numb and stiff from the cold.

The barbershop was busy with all of the waiting area chairs filled and people standing up. Charles stood near the door and waited his turn. After a long anxious wait, Charles climbed up into the red leather chair, which was promptly ratcheted upward. The barber, a middle-aged man with a prominent potbelly, began humming a tune to himself as he started clipping away. Charles looked down at the nickel-plated footrest and studied the Adolph Koch scroll. The barber had been clipping with the scissors for only a minute when he got out the electric shaver and began to mow what he had missed from the neck on up. The humming volume increased to compensate for the buzz of the shaver until two minutes later when Charles jumped off the chair. He handed the contented barber the quarter and received a shiny new penny in return. "That's for you, sonny," the barber said, breaking his tune for a moment. Then he started humming again and turned around for his next customer.

On the way out of the barbershop Charles passed a man sitting in a waiting room chair. The man had his finger stuck in his ear. Charles looked back. The finger was stuck into the ear as if he was scratching out ear wax or satisfying an itch. His finger however was stuck in until only the last knuckle showed. The man looked at Charles and grinned. Charles stared, wondering how the man could get three inches of finger jammed into his ear. Maybe he has a hole in his ear, he thought and cringed at a worse idea. Or maybe an earwig ate a hole in his ear. The other men in the barbershop saw Charles staring and started to chuckle. As Charles walked out the door some of them broke out laughing loudly. The barber turned around as the man took his finger out of his ear and held it up for everybody to see. It had been shot off in the middle in combat during the War.

"Walter, are you playing your old trick on the children again?" the barber announced loudly in case anybody had missed the event, before he guffawed with the rest of the audience.

The movie theatre was farther down the street. As Charles walked he rubbed the back of his neck where it was itching from the hasty removal of all his hair. The only good thing about the barber was he took so much hair off that it would be a long time before Charles needed to go back again. The movie would not start for an hour yet. When Charles arrived, a line had already formed and extended out to the edge of the building. Charles joined the line and began waiting again. After a wait that seemed forever, the line, which now snaked around to the back of the building, began to move. Inside the theatre Charles stood in another line at the boys' restroom, a line leading to a water fountain, and then another line at the candy and popcorn counter. Eventually he got to a seat in the theatre. The place was filled with a restless mob of jabbering kids. Charles ate his popcorn in silence. At last the lights went out and the movie started.

The theatre had reduced the double feature to a single show this week because of the immensely popular Bambi movie by Walt Disney. It was the most popular movie ever shown by any movie house outside of "Gone With The Wind." It was also in Technicolor. Charles watched in fascination at the detailed animation as the deer grew up. He wondered why Bambi had no father. As in his own life the mother had the whole job of raising the children. Near the end of the movie the father deer suddenly appeared to lead Bambi out of danger. Tears welled up in Charles' eyes as he realized that the father had been around all the time to watch over Bambi and that he was a strong and magnificent stag. A king of the forest. Charles still had tears in his eyes when Bambi had grown up to be a stag like his father and the movie ended.

On the long walk home that afternoon Charles kept thinking of the excitement and richness of the movie and how the tragedies and family upbringing of a deer could somehow parallel the lives of real people. After all, he saw a lot of his mother and very little of his father. He even talked like his mother, who grew up in a different place than his father. He was glad that his life was not as dangerous as the deer family's.

The next day Charles went next door to meet Mary Anne to walk to church together. Nobody was home. Charles belatedly remembered they had gone to the country the day before. 'They probably stayed overnight,' he reasoned. 'Darn, I hate going to church without Mary Anne.' He trudged off to church near the town square alone pocketing his offering of ten cents. His parents never went to church. They were religious, that is they believed in God, but they never bothered to go to the church. They felt it was important, however, that Charles go to church so that he would grow up with the right principles and religion. Charles carried the Bible that was given to him at his baptism.

After church Charles came home to find his father working in the garden area of the yard. The yard was divided into two halves. One half had two large trees, an apple tree and an old elm, with a cesspool poking through the ground near the side fence. The other half was an open area which would be transformed into a garden each year. At one end of it, in permanent residence, was rhubarb which would ultimately be pulled and sweetened into pie filling. The back-fence border was a row of flowers which would grow back into full bloom each year. In this area, after the earth had warmed, small bleeding-heart plants would sprout up while in between small stalks of lily of the valley would show their small bells in descending sizes. The flower territory belonged to Mother, the garden was Father's.

Charles ran into the house, changed and went out to help his father. He was looking forward to working with him. The whole garden area had been spaded and turned over during the morning while Charles was at church. Tom saw Charles and grinned. Charles smiled back asking:

"Father, what are we growing in the Victory Garden this year?"

Tom pointed to a pile of long thin pointed sticks.

"We're growin' string beans. But nary as big as the ones in the Jack and the Beanstalk tale. I figger with your help we can be finished before dark. It'll do you some good 'n keep you from gettin' in your mother's way. More'n that, you can learn how to work the earth. All good on this earth comes from the ground. That's something they don't teach you in Sunday School. Drop a seed in each hole and cover it over," he advised as he handed Charles a bag of seed beans.

"I hate string beans." Charles announced with a sour face as he picked up the bag.

Tom carefully poked holes in the rocky soil with Charles following in tow dropping a bean in each and filling it in. An hour later there were twenty rows of carefully patted mounds. Then they started over with Charles holding bean poles steady while Tom pounded them with a heavy square machinist's hammer. Sometimes a stick would be driven into a rock underground and would bend when struck. Charles would then pull it out and move it a few inches away. They worked all afternoon until the pile of sticks was used up. Charles noticed that his father was not tired when they were finished. There were no blisters on Tom's hands from digging up the earth or hammering away all afternoon. Charles had a few splinters in his tender hands. He did not say anything about them because he did not want his father to think he was a sissy. He also noticed that his father's hands were impervious to splinters because they were so hard and calloused from years of work.

That night he wanted to go out to sell more seeds but his mother would not let him.

"Let the poor people have a peaceful Sunday evening," Rose said.

Dinner was succotash, which he hated because the beans and corn were out of cans. Rose told him it was Indian food but he didn't believe her. 'Indians must have lived a terrible life if they had to eat this,' he thought. Afterward he lay on the living room floor reading the newspaper comic strips. As soon as he finished his father picked it up to read the adventures of Prince Valiant.

The next day after school Charles was out selling his seeds again. He went to a different part of town and found that nobody there went to his school. The results were better. He traveled over unfamiliar streets until it was dark and he was very tired. He returned home and counted his money. There was almost $25.00 now. That had to be a record. By the end of the week he had collected another dollar. He was sure to win a prize with $25.80 in sales.

Friday was the big day. All the children brought their seed lists and money. There were some discrepancies between the lists and the money. The teacher adjusted the lists so that they added up properly.

"Children, I hope you kept a list of the people who bought your seeds so you'll know who gets them," she reminded. Charles had been so busy selling the seeds that he hadn't bothered to make any list. He had also been all over town to sell them and most of the people he saw were strangers. He began to worry about how to distribute the seeds he would receive next week.

The teacher was all smiles. This was the greatest sale yet. She tallied up the sales by student. Some of the students had done very well. She decided to award three prizes instead of one. The first prize of a silver dollar went to a girl named Susan. She had sold $27.10 worth of seeds. The dark-haired girl had been telling her classmates that she had been to a wedding the weekend before and had found everybody in a generous mood to buy her seeds. Her mother had looked the other way as she wove through the crowd with her brochure, pencil and little red snap purse in hand. The second prize went to Charles. He was elated and ran up to the front of the class to collect. His prize was a small pearl-handled jackknife with two blades. He went back to his seat opening and shutting the blades as he sat down. The third prize was a collection of Christopher Columbus' ships with, Pinta, Nina, and the Santa Maria, names painted with tiny letters on the masts. They were made of walnut halves with matchstick masts and paper sails. They were colorfully painted and had "Made in Occupied Japan" stamped on the bottom in miniature letters. The girl who won them had sold $11.80 in seeds to relatives and friends.

A week later the seeds were distributed. Charles brought his big box home.

"Do you have the list of customers to give them to?" His mother asked. Charles's face turned red as he didn't answer. Rose was about to ask him again when she realized that he had no list. "Did you lose it?" she asked again.

"No," Charles answered sheepishly, "I forgot to make it."

His mother's first reaction was anger. "Charles, how could you be so dumb!"

'How is he going to get the seeds back to those people?' she thought. After a minute her mood changed to humor. 'The boy was so busy selling them that he entirely forgot to do it. Now he has all those packages of seeds and will have to figure out who to give them to.' She put her arm around his shoulders and led him into the living room to devise a plan of distribution. Looking at Charles, she grinned and wagged her head. Charles's face was crimson and he didn't dare say a word.

After school the next week Charles made the rounds of his neighborhood distributing the seeds as best he could. Then he tried the other neighborhoods but gave up after a futile attempt at a few houses. His mother planted the largest flower bed in town between the side lawn and Tom's garden. Most of the lawn was dug up by Tom with Charles' reluctant assistance the following week. A magnificent spread of dozens of different flowers representing the full spectrum of the brochure came into bloom after a short incubation of spring sunshine and warmth. Afterward people would go out of their way to visit and admire the magnificent array. Rose would look out the window and see the admirers and smile to herself. 'If they only knew,' she would think to herself.

One-night Charles had trouble sleeping. He was tossing and turning in bed until late in the night. In his troubled sleep he dreamed of a huge clock in the sky. The clock filled the whole sky with nothing else to be seen. Instead of 60 minutes, the clock was numbered in quarters—25, 50, 75, and 100 at the top. It was a metric clock like the one he had imagined at school. A giant hand pointing straight at the top started to move slowly in a clockwise fashion. As it moved the arrow of the hand changed into a baby. The baby waved it's arms up and down. As the hand progressed to the right quarter the baby changed into a small boy. The boy smiled as he grew. Then he proceeded to grow tall and thin as a young man. The hand kept moving down and the young man grew older and heavier. The look on his face became very serious and concerned. When the hand moved into the final quarter the man was much older with pure white hair. The pain was evident in his features. The hand kept moving until the fragile man suddenly appeared lifeless. The hand stopped at 100. The hand started to turn again. The baby was there as before with different clothes. The face and movement was the same. Charles began to recognize the child in the clock. It was the same child in the pictures that his mother had taken of him with the Kodak Brownie. Charles woke up. He stared wide-eyed at the ceiling of his little room. He got up to get a drink of water from the bathroom. Charles didn't understand the clock of life he had just dreamed. He got the drink and returned to bed. Frightened by the mysterious dream, he decided he wouldn't tell anybody about his strange dream. After a troubled hour he went back to sleep.

Chapter Five

Buttercups

The school year was ending in several weeks. The children were getting restless. By the end of each day in school, the entire classroom was squirming like a can of worms. After the milk and sandwich break, fresh air would sweep through the open windows, electrifying all the children. A strong smell of plant life growing outside permeated the air. The pine pitch mixed with maple and oak in the upper air while the lower ground was filled with grasses and wildflowers of the nearby field and woods. There was little that Miss Pritchett could do to hold her children's attention. She tried various devices, such as bringing in her National Geographic and Life magazines for a diversion, but by the end of the day she was back to where she started. The children could not escape, so the contest for attention continued as the weather turned from warm to hot.

On the way home the children were loud and animated. There was a surplus of energy which had been stored during the long winter months. Soon school would be out and there would be more time to play. While being herded home one sunny day Charles was talking to Mary Anne about going to church the coming Sunday.

"Aren't all churches the same?" Charles asked.

Mary Anne thought a minute and tried to dredge up something from Sunday School or home. She had only half an answer.

"I think that all Protestant religions are the same. There is a lady down the street who is Catholic and she has statues of Mary and Jesus all over the house. I think their religion is different." She looked at Charles trying to decide what he was thinking.

"I don't mean the different religions. My mother said that all religions believe in God. What I'm wondering is if you go to the Congregational Church every Sunday and they have sermons and sing hymns and have Sunday School afterward and since my Baptist Church does the same thing, aren't they really the same church?" Charles had compared notes with Mary Anne many times on Sundays as they walked to church together. The only difference that he could see was that his church baptized him later than hers did. Outside of that, the rest of the Sunday service was pretty much the same.

Mary Anne pondered the statement.

"Gosh, Charles, if you want to know, why don't you go to church with me next Sunday? Then you can see what we do there. I'm sure they won't mind because the minister always tells everybody to bring their friends and neighbors." She smiled at her solution. If Charles went with her, he would also be able to walk her home again. She liked going to church with Charles but hated coming home alone. It was a very long walk. Besides, maybe he would like her church better than his.

"That's a great idea. I'm tired of my church anyway. I'll go with you if you promise me one thing."

"What do I have to do?"

"Just go with me to my church next week and we'll know what happens at both places." Charles was happy. He found church very boring. The sermons were for grown people because the minister always discussed the various ways to sin and what would happen if they did. He liked Sunday School and always found the Bible stories interesting. Perhaps because they were great examples of the terrible things that happened to people when they did sin.

Mary Anne started thinking of what her mother would say if she found out that she was not in her church. She did not want to tell her mother in case she would not approve of the exchange. On the other hand, maybe, the minister or Sunday School teacher would miss her and call to see why she was not attending. The idea of visiting Charles' church was interesting though.

"I'll go with you just one time, Charles," she said. "If I go more than that my mother will find out and I'll get in trouble."

The plan was set for the next Sunday.

On the way to school the next morning Charles smelled flowers. It was not the usual strong smell of flowers like the big flower garden that had suddenly sprung up outside his house. It was light, faintly sweet and overwhelming to the senses. He had never swelled anything so good. It was as if the walkway to school had been bathed in perfume which had been diluted by the sun and wind. He looked across the street to find the source. Where the hill joined the field a belt of grass continued along the road. Charles saw a large patch of bright yellow beyond the grass.

"Do you see the yellow flowers?" he asked Mary Anne as he pointed to the yellow patch.

"Yes," she answered. "I just love flowers. Gosh, those look wonderful. I have an idea. Let's go see them after school today."

Charles agreed.

The school day had been no less agonizing than usual and as soon as he finished and got home Charles changed his clothes and found Mary Anne waiting outside for him.

She had woven her blonde hair in pigtails. Her mother had dressed her in a faded red dress that showed her knees as she outgrew it. Her mother saved things. Nothing was ever thrown away until it was totally useless or nobody else could wear it. Like Charles' playclothes, her worn brown and white saddle shoes had been her dress shoes the year before. Skinny white arms protruded from the shoulders of the dress. This was the first time she had worn the dress outside this year because of the winter cold. They went skipping and running off to the field near the school.

Instead of walking on the sidewalk they went across the street and along the woods. They came to the stream and stopped.

"Let's go to the waterfall," Charles suggested.

Mary Anne shouted:

"Catch me if you can!" And started running up the hill.

Five minutes later they were looking up at a column of water that sprouted out of a crack in the granite cliff above. It fell twenty-five feet to a stone basin and coursed over a zigzag route until it went under the street. The water was cold and clear. They sat down at the pool near the bottom of the fall. Charles scooped some water into his cupped hands and drank. It tasted pure and good. Mary Anne did the same. They sat there for a few minutes looking at the water. There was no life in it. No fish, no frogs, nothing grew in the pure shallow pool of rushing water.

They resumed their walk through the woods to get to the other side of the hill. As they reached the top of the hill, they entered a sparse area with a large briar thicket.

"That's a briar patch where the rabbits go!" Mary Anne exclaimed. "Can you see the path that goes into the briars?"

Sure enough, there was a path that led to a tunnel into the base of the thicket of thorns. They walked around and saw more tunnels into it. No rabbits were visible today.

They followed, hand in hand, one of the paths that led to the briar patch from the other side. It was narrow and sometimes went through bushes but kept clear of the rocks and trees that were scattered over the hillside. They climbed over a low overgrown stone wall made of rocks piled on one another. The wall had no beginning and no end. It rambled into view from the street and out of sight over the nearest hill.

Finally, they were looking out at a field of solid yellow buttercups.

"Gosh, it's beautiful!" Mary Anne exclaimed as she ran into the meadow. A golden carpet of buttercups stretched as far as the eye could see. It was a once-in-a-lifetime view of opulence. A king could have his diamonds and gold but the children had a field of beauty. They ran through it until they were breathless. Charles stopped running and sat down. Mary Anne joined him. He pulled a few flowers from the carpet and studied them. The yellow pollen and petals left a stain on his fingers. Then he pulled some more and rubbed them on the back of Mary Anne's hand. She did the same to him.

The warm sun beat down on the children as they rolled and played in the golden flowerbed. A spring breeze bathed them in an essence of perfumed air and the warmth of a new season. The remainder of the afternoon passed swiftly.

Charles felt relaxed and at peace with the world. He was very happy. He and Mary Anne were covered with buttercup gold. They had painted each other's arms and legs with it.

"Mary Anne?" Charles asked meekly as he watched her happy face.

"What, Charles?" she answered as she shooed a bee away from her trodden space in the sea of flowers.

"Will you be my girlfriend always and marry me when we grow up?" It was easy to say because he was as close to Mary Anne as his sister. Probably more so because he could not share things with his sister because she was older than him. Charles was happy and wanted assurance that nothing would ever change. Deep inside Charles was afraid of the changes from growing up and wanted Mary Anne to stay close to him and share the changes with him. He could not afford to have her leave with the changes. He knew she loved him as much as her little sister but he had never talked to her about it before.

Mary Anne held his hand and looked at the little boy. There was nobody else in her small world. There was no contest for affection. She felt no desire except for somebody nice and close to talk and share things with. He was as important as her family. She loved him as much as her parents and her little sister. It was easy to tell Charles.

"Of course, Charles, I'll always love you," she said as she squeezed his hand. "I'd be awful lonely if you weren't next door to me all the time when I need a friend. Someday when we get grown up it would be nice to be married and have our own family." Her pale blue eyes grew dreamy as she thought of pushing a baby carriage with her baby instead of a doll in it. She suddenly threw her arms around him and they rolled over and over in the flowers.

"I'm glad," Charles said. He would have been devastated if she had said anything different. The mutuality of feeling between them was reassuring. He was radiantly happy. This was the greatest day of his life. Everything about the day was beautiful. He felt the closeness to nature and other people that the Indians must have known before the invasion of the Europeans.

"I have a secret I haven't told anybody in the world before now." Charles stated. "I know you think I'm crazy but I think I can make a hundred-minute metric hour and create time for just me."

Mary Anne looked at Charles. "Are you talking about that silly metric clock again? You'll get in trouble thinking like that."

Charles tried explaining again. "Listen, if my clock has 100 minutes and I use 60 for ordinary things, I can have 40 minutes left for special things like when I want to daydream and escape from whatever I am doing. Don't you ever want to shut off the world and do something special in your own time when nobody can bother you?

"Charles, sometimes you're too complicated for me. I'm glad you told me your secret but I don't really understand you. I'll promise not to tell anybody about your silly clock, though."

The sun rested on the horizon. Long shadows reached out from the trees on the edge of the meadow. The sky turned a crimson red at the edge of the world as the waning light filtered through the prismatic atmosphere.

Charles and Mary Anne hastily fled home hand in hand to escape the darkness. They knew their parents would not understand how they got the yellow gold all over their clothes and skin. They knew they were in trouble.

When Charles' mother asked him about the yellow stain on his clothes and skin he mumbled something unintelligible and disappeared into the kitchen to turn the radio on. He looked so happy that she did not bother to ask anymore. She had been a child once and remembered that silly look when she had done something that made her happy but her parents did not approve of. A punishment at this time was of no value. Punishment of capital offenses was left to his father. When he had done something terrible like lighting a fire in the backyard one day, his father had taken his belt to him. Tom was awful mad that day saying, "I'll whip him until the cows come home!" She could forgive many little things knowing that he would be well taken care of if he did something bad enough.

That Sunday Charles walked into the great stone church near the town square. Mary Anne was at his side. He felt lost in the crowd of big people as they filed in and filled the pews. They sat together as the preacher recited a quotation from the Bible about being sinful with the neighbor's wife instead of your own. Then he quoted the commandment about the same. The sermon followed about temptation and the opportunity to go to Hell. Charles and Mary Anne grinned at one another. She put her hand over her mouth at one time to hold back a giggle. Finally, they stood up with the worshipers to sing hymns. Their weak voices were indistinguishable in the dense crowd of grownups. When the collection tray arrived they both dropped ten cents in it and passed it on. Sunday School was more fun, with some colored papers depicting the Jews' flight from Egypt and the matching discussion about Moses' trials with the Pharaoh.

The next week they went to Charles' church. The sermon was very lively as the minister discussed stealing money and cheating people out of things they owned. It was not as interesting as stealing another man's wife. At any rate the Lord would forgive thieves as he did when he was crucified. Charles reasoned that people had to be caught before they could be forgiven. After singing and Sunday School, Charles asked Mary Anne if his church was any better than hers.

"They're both dull except Sunday School," she said. After that they returned to their former routine of going to their old churches alone, even though their parents never found out.

One afternoon Mary Anne asked Charles to visit her house after school. "Hurry! I have a surprise!" she said, all excited.

Charles went to the house with her on the way home. Mary Anne took Charles by the hand and led him into her bedroom. She was all smiles as she pointed to the walls. "Look what my mother and I have done!"

The walls were covered with bright red strawberries. A stem and bright green leaves were attached to each. They were uniformly distributed and each strawberry was almost identical to the next down to the dimpled dots that broke up the solid red of the berries.

"Wow, those are fantastic!" Charles exclaimed, "They look just like wallpaper! They look even better than wallpaper because they have nicer colors."

"I wouldn't let my mother paint the walls and we couldn't afford wallpaper so we decided to paint the strawberries. It took us more than a month to finish. Father got a string and marked it for the strawberries. And he marked the walls so that we put the strawberries in the right place. Mother drew the strawberries and I helped her paint them in. I painted all of the green leaves and stems, while she painted the red part and the dots. Aren't they beautiful?"

Charles agreed with her while wondering why he couldn't do the same for his room. Perhaps something better or more interesting like the great whale Moby Dick. When he got home later he told his mother what Mary Anne and her family had done. Then he asked her if he could do something to his room and she told him that Mary Anne was much more talented than Charles or his family.

"Nobody here has the kind of patience to do something that artistic," Rose declared, as she went on with her housekeeping.

That evening Charles lay in bed thinking about the strawberries. In his mind he created the Metric Clock and allocated his forty minutes to painting Moby Dick whales on the walls of his room. He had painted one whole wall before time ran out and he was sound asleep.

Summer

Chapter Six

Going Fishing

$\mathscr{E}$very evening that week Rose read a chapter of Moby Dick to Charles before he went to bed. He would lie in bed afterward thinking about the power of the giant animals of the sea and the men who spent their lives conquering them. The mysterious story left Charles absolutely intrigued. One evening he asked his mother how big a whale was.

"Oh," she exclaimed, trying to keep in the spirit of the story, "at least 50 feet long. They're gigantic creatures. Remember the Bible story where Jonah was swallowed by a whale and lived inside for a while until the whale threw him up again?"

Charles looked up at her with bewilderment.

"Gosh, how big is fifty feet?" he asked. "Is it as big as the space between the backyard trees?"

"Yes, certainly," his mother answered. She started reading again. A little while later she finished for the evening and Charles was left alone with his thoughts. He went to sleep trying to fit the whale into the known dimensions of things around him such as the house, the backyard, and the schoolyard where he played ball.

The next morning, he went directly out to the backyard. He walked under the clothesline and went straight to the big apple tree. The Macintosh tree had seen better days and for the past few years had been ignored and left to produce bad fruit and carry some unpruned dead limbs. The wormy fruit was allowed to go unpicked until it fell to the ground. Small woolly caterpillar cocoons nested between the branches to contaminate this year's crop. Charles paced the distance between the apple tree and the old elm tree in the back of the yard. He completed twenty steps walking widely. He was not sure how many feet it was. He knew it was more than a foot a step, but he was not certain if it was fifty or more. At any rate, he concluded, no whale would be bigger than that.

Adam suddenly came around the corner of the house with his big brown shaggy dog trotting next to him. Adam's father called him Moocher because he was always hungry and would eat anything. His mother called it a League of Nations dog because it had obviously mixed nationalities. Adam called him Rex because he liked the name. Adam let people know that his dog was the friendliest creature in town because Rex's tail was always wagging. Once he told Charles that people should have tails so other people would know what kind of mood they were in. And if people were as friendly as his dog the world would be a better place to live in.

"Hey, what are you doing?" Adam asked as he switched a small branch he trimmed off a bush on the way over.

"I'm trying to figure out how big a whale is. Don't you think a whale is as big as the place between the trees?"

"Naw," Adam answered, "whales are just made to look bigger in the movies than they really are. After all, hunters kill them with spears just like other animals, the same as elephants." He wasn't concerned with how big a dumb whale was. He wanted to go fishing.

"Charles, I just found out about a great place to go fishing. We can't tell our folks about it because it's a secret place. My Uncle Walter told me about it when he was visiting Sunday. Let's go today?"

Charles' eyes lit up. He loved to go fishing, although he never caught anything. He remembered one-day last summer when he went fishing with his sister and her boyfriend. His mother had insisted he go to see that the couple behaved. The boyfriend had helped him bait his hook and was very nice to him. He was especially nice to his sister and was kissing her madly all afternoon. They also talked a lot and by the end of the day nobody had caught any fish. Before they left a man with a tin bucket came and threw out a line from the shore. He did not use a fishing rod or anything fancy. Just a line. Then he started pulling in fat black squiggly eels one after another until the bucket was full. When they left it was dark and the man also left with his bucket of eels still wiggling. Charles asked his sister what the man would do with the eels and did not believe her answer that people eat them. He also could not figure out how the man could catch a bucket of eels as easily as that. Charles added the experience to the list of mysteries that he would have to solve sooner or later.

"Sure, I'll go. I'll dig some worms if you get the other kids." Charles volunteered knowing that it would be unthinkable to not let the others in on the trip.

"Okay I'll be back as soon as I can." Adam said, already on his way. Charles ran into the house and told Rose that he was going fishing with the kids.

"You can go but be real careful. I don't want to hear you drowned or did something foolish," she said perfunctorily. She always worried about him when he was gone. Rose wished there was more that she could do with him. "Be a good boy. Next week we'll take the bus and go to the beach together." With that statement she went back to her ironing with the flatiron in one hand and the sprinkling bottle in the other.

Charles started digging worms near the cesspool. He hated the cesspool with its rusty brown cast-iron cover. He usually walked well around it when he was in the yard. Sometimes a stink would come from it. He knew what was in it and imagined a death worse than any he had seen in the movies would happen if he ever fell into it. There were lots of worms to be had there because sometimes the liquid overflowed on to the ground keeping it moist and fertile. By the time he dug a tin can half full of the crawly critters he was tired. He rested and a few minutes later Harry, Merle, and Adam arrived with gear in hand.

"Adam, you'll have to leave your dog behind," Merle was saying. "He'll bark and get us in trouble."

"Darn, you're no fun. He goes everywhere with me. Maybe he can help us catch a rabbit or something," he responded seriously.

"Ha, ha," Harry countered, "My mother says that your mutt couldn't track an elephant over a newly plowed field."

Adam turned and ran for home with the dog following. "Be sure and wait for me!" he yelled over his shoulder.

Charles went into the house to get his fishing pole and cigar box with hooks and sinkers. When he came back into the yard, Harry and Merle were jumping up and down with excitement over something Adam was doing. Charles walked past them as Adam yelled:

"Watch out!"

Adam reached out with his switch and whipped a huge caterpillar cobweb. The switch made swishing noises as it bit into the web time and time again. Pieces of the web and leaves from the tree flew into the air along with two-inch-long black baby caterpillars. After a few minutes the web was demolished. The kids stomped the caterpillars which were crawling all over the ground where they landed. The boys delighted in making green spots on the ground where the caterpillars were crushed. Adam found another web and started whipping it. An hour passed until the last of the cobwebs near ground level had been attacked. The ground was littered with green spots from deceased caterpillars. The bottoms of the boys' shoes were green with the crushed remains. Adam threw his switch away. It was green from the caterpillars he whipped on the tree trunk and branches after the webs were gone. Everybody was excited. The day was off to a great start.

A square of boys headed to the secret fishing hole. "We have to be careful and not get caught," Adam was saying. "My uncle said if we get caught we can go to jail."

"Wait a minute!" Harry exclaimed. "My mother won't let me go any place that can get me in trouble. You didn't tell me it was dangerous."

"Gosh, it's not dangerous. The problem is that the fishpond is located in the cemetery. We have to trespass to get there. My uncle said there are giant goldfish there because nobody is ever allowed to catch them." He grinned with excitement as he held his hands up to show what size a giant goldfish would be.

"Goldfish don't grow into big fish," Harry said as the party stopped to debate. "I can't go with you because it's wrong. Besides, there couldn't be giant goldfish in any pond." He knew that there were only baby goldfish that grew up to be larger little goldfish in fishbowls in people's houses. He turned around and started walking home. "Is anybody coming back with me?" he asked, half-expecting the expedition to collapse.

It did not. The boys were anxious to know if there really were giant goldfish in the world. Especially if they could catch them and bring some back home. Merle and Charles followed Adam toward the town square and the secret place.

"Where's Richard?" Charles asked, noticing that one member of the gang was missing.

"He got sent off to live with his grandmother for the summer," Merle replied. He had just been getting used to the new kid on the street when he disappeared for the whole summer.

The boys headed down Main Street toward the town hall. After a long tiring hike, they sat down to rest.

"Are you sure there's really a fishpond where we're going?" Merle asked. He heard his father talk about trout fishing in the mountains but never about giant goldfish.

Adam was positive it was not very far away. He reassured them:

"Don't worry about where we're going. I won't mislead you. I'm pretty sure I know where to find the cemetery. I had to go there once before when a relative died." He vividly remembered that day. They had ridden to the funeral parlor with other people in a big black Buick that had a hood at least ten feet long. He didn't even know which relative was dead. It was a miserable day with people standing around everywhere. The women were all crying, or pretending to cry. The men just looked sad and talked among themselves. There was an old man playing the organ in the funeral parlor. He hated the organ. It was worse than the one he heard in church on Sundays. The cemetery had lots of grass and trees. He remembered the birds singing in the trees. They were everywhere. One of them crapped on a man's shoulder. It just fell out of the tree and landed on his dark blue woolen pin-striped suit. Adam remembered grinning as the man wiped at it with his handkerchief while scowling at the bird overhead. As everybody left Adam wondered who got to fill in the hole. 'What if they forget?' he speculated. 'Then somebody could sneak back and steal the body from the open grave.'

The trek resumed and an hour after they passed through the town square they suddenly encountered a high stone wall. The wall was taller than Adam, the tallest boy, and went a long way down the street—as far as the eye could see.

"Hooray, at last we're here! We have to turn here and follow the wall to the back so nobody can see us," Adam advised as they neared the barrier.

They turned following the wall into the woods on the side of the road. Nobody talked now. They were afraid of getting caught. This wall was six feet tall and had been built during the Depression. For some reason, when everybody was out of work there was enough money from people dying to construct a cemetery wall and gardens large enough to last the rest of the century. The cemetery had a large stone Catholic Church in front of it. Only Adam had ever been to this church, the rest of the boys had not known of its existence because it was beyond the range of their travels and exploration. The oldest graves had been filled nearest the church and over the years the cemetery expanded to rear areas. This enlargement had provided roads and rose gardens out of the way where the priests and nuns could relax and meditate. A small chapel there provided shelter and comfort for funeral services when the church was in use for other functions. Granite crypts lined one side of the yard nearest the church. Over the years additional crypts had been built until a row of them now extended into the back of the cemetery opposite the wall the children would scale to enter. In the middle of the garden was a very large pond which had been stocked with goldfish and claimed by wild ducks. At a later time, a pair of swans was donated. It was a most peaceful place to be. Over the years the slender trees grew tall and the fish grew larger.

The boys reached the rear of the wall and after a great effort scaled it to the other side.

"Wow!" Merle exclaimed when he saw the parklike setting of well-kept winding roads, trees and endless lawn. "Look at the tombstones!" he added as he pointed to the neat rows of headstones leading towards Main Street. They spotted the pond at the back of the park and walked along the wall towards it. The boys were uneasy as they watched for witnesses. They were also nervous at being in a graveyard. They didn't like being around the ghosts of all the people buried there. The pond had bushes along the wall to hide it from visitors. The boys kept going until they were between the wall and the bushes.

"Let's hide in the bushes so we won't get caught," Charles whispered. Without waiting to see what the other boys did, he crawled into a big bush. The bush had a large space under the branches where he was invisible. Charles looked up and saw the other boys had disappeared into other bushes. Within a few minutes three handlines were suspended on the water by cork bobbers. Charles looked into the water and saw several large fat goldfish almost a foot-long glide into view. His heart pounded with excitement. He wanted to yell to the other boys but was afraid to. He crawled to the nearest bush to inform Merle. Merle had seen one of the fish and was as excited as Charles was. Charles went back to his hiding place to resume fishing.

The summer heat beat down on the children. They had forgotten to bring any water with them. The pond water was not appealing enough to drink. The boys were not used to being away from home for long periods.

The fish were not biting. They would lazily swim within sight of the boys but were not hungry. Charles found himself replacing grey drowned worms frequently with live ones from his can. Every now and then one of the boys would crawl over and take a supply of worms. Charles was getting mad. 'This is a waste of time to come so far and look the fish in the eye just so I can drown worms,' he thought.

Suddenly there was a loud splashing near the bank in front of a bush. Adam yelled:

"Hey gang, I've got one!" while he pulled in a large fighting fish. As he lifted it out of the water he yelled again, "It's a big one!"

Charles met Merle coming out of his bush as they went over to see what Adam was bringing in. Adam was staring with disbelief at a large three-pound fish on the end of his line.

Adam tried taking the hook out of its mouth, with Charles and Merle holding the slippery fish, when there was a noise at the other side of the pond.

At the end of the afternoon several priests decided to take a walk through the garden to enjoy the fresh air. They had been in the church reading and meditating. A change was welcomed. The church was cool in the mornings but would heat up in the afternoon as the sun came through the windows and finally around the stone walls. When they got past the area where the tombstones ended they heard a noise and a child's voice. They headed for the noise and found loud voices coming from a bush on the other side of the pond.

"Somebody is at our pond!" one of the priests exclaimed as he ran toward it.

"They've seen us!" Adam yelled as he scrambled out of his bush. The other boys followed and a mad dash ensued to the end of the wall.

Charles tripped and fell. As he got, up one of the priests was close enough to reach out and touch his shirt. He ran like a madman to reach the wall. They got to the wall with the priests close behind yelling for them to stop. The boys scurried over the wall and ran straight into the woods before they stopped.

"Did anybody follow us over the wall?" Merle asked, panting between breaths.

"I didn't see them come over," Adam answered.

The boys sat down next to a big rock not saying a word for a full five minutes. Charles got up and looked around. Nobody had followed them.

"Wow! Did you see how big my fish was?" Adam asked, knowing they had all seen and handled his fish.

"Gosh, that was really funny," Charles said, as he started laughing hysterically. "You catch the biggest goldfish in the world and we nearly get caught by a bunch of priests in black robes."

With that the children laughed loudly as their nervousness wore off.

"Darn, all of my fishing gear is lost," Merle stated. "What am I going to tell my mother when I get home?"

He was not alone. None of the boys had salvaged any of their gear when they left so hastily. The fishing rods, lines, sinkers, hooks, and bobbers were under the three bushes at the edge of the pond.

"Maybe we can go back for our stuff after dark." Adam suggested.

"You're crazy." Charles countered. "I'm not going into any cemetery in the dark. Especially with the priests looking for us. Besides, our parents will never let us go out at night."

"This place is too far away to come back for the gear. We're lucky to still be alive with all of those people chasing us," Merle joined in. "We'd better think of a good story to tell our parents when we get home."

They resumed the long walk home. Nobody came up with any suggestions until they passed the town square.

"Why tell our parents anything?" Adam suggested. "They'll never know what happened."

"No sir, my parents would find out right away," Merle stated. "My Dad will ask me all kinds of questions about the trip. If he sees I have no gear he'll get suspicious. I could tell him that it all fell in the water but he'd want to know why I didn't wade in and get it out. Sometimes it's hard to fool my old man. Especially about things like fishing."

"Maybe we can tell them we were robbed by somebody with a gun and he took everything we had." Charles was letting his imagination take charge of him. "We could say he tried to kidnap us but we escaped."

Adam thought a moment and had the solution. "That's stupid. I have a better idea. Let's say that a gang of kids beat us up and took all of our gear. He thought a moment about the lack of evidence such as torn clothes and bruises from a fight. "At least we can say a gang was going to beat us up to take our money and gear."

The other boys agreed on the bully story, and although a description of the members of the gang was not uniformly agreed to, they were in agreement that they were outnumbered and that the bullies were all older and bigger than them.

The boys got home at dusk very tired, thirsty and hungry. They all had a common tale about catching a big fish but losing it and their gear to some big boys who almost beat them up.

Charles' mother did not know what parts of his story to believe. "I hope you learn to take care of yourself someday," she said as he wiped a milky mustache on his sleeve. "The next time you go away for the whole day you had better take a lunch and something to drink."

Charles grinned knowing that he would not go back to the fishpond with or without a lunch. That evening he sat on the back porch reviewing the exciting day. Stars filled the sky overhead. The evening breeze was relaxing. He closed his eyes and saw his metric clock. With his allocated special time he imagined being back at the pond and reeling in dozens of golden fish. They were even bigger than the one that Adam caught. He was placing one in a big pile under the bush when he felt a hand on his shoulder as his father announced his bedtime.

Chapter Seven

Learning to Smoke

With the school vacation came sultry summer heat and boredom. Bands of children roved the streets in search of a solution to twelve-hour school-less days. At first there was a long list of events and desires carried about in the mind of each child. As summer started up, the list quickly became exhausted. A new burden was placed on mothers to find things for the children to do and to keep from tripping over them when they hung around the house. Endless weeks of anticipated summer fun were replaced with boredom. The children were learning that, as with many things, their predetermined events became altered subjectively by parents and uncontrollable circumstance.

Charles wandered about his backyard daily, exploring the changes in every nook and cranny. The beansprouts were now thin vines that snaked up hundreds of tall sticks in the garden quarter. Small springy tendrils wrapped themselves around the poles as the vines advanced higher and higher. Bright green leaves covered the vines with skinny bean shoots becoming noticeable. Due to a lack of rain Charles watered the plants every morning with a garden hose. Because he was a quiet person he enjoyed the solitude while studying the garden as he wet it down.

The flower garden was in full bloom. There were always cut flowers scattered about the house in various vases from an endless supply. As flowers wilted and died, others would spring up larger and stronger to take their place. The colorful garden was alive with life.

In the backyard a delicate row of lily of the valley, and the larger red bleeding-heart plants lined the fence from end to end. Charles was sure to allow extra watering time for these flowers because they were his mother's favorites and he could not let them wilt or die from neglect.

The apple tree now had small green apples. There were more than apples; because if you looked carefully, there also were long fuzzy black caterpillars moving about with their vacuum feet attacking the leaves and the remaining apple blossoms. Every house in the neighborhood had at least one apple or Bartlett pear tree in the backyard. They also shared the caterpillars.

There was an arbor attached to the rear of the house. The latticework was covered with bright green leaves as grapevines came to life. Small green pea-sized grapes appeared in clusters amid the leaves. The arbor provided some shade for the back of the house. When the purple grapes would finally ripen they would be too sour to eat. The family was not sophisticated enough to make wine with them.

The elm tree in the rear of the yard now had a rope tied around a large dead branch. From the rope hung an old tire from the gas station on Main Street. Tom put the tire swing up for Charles one free Sunday. Some summers before, Charles had spent many hours with a small round metal sifter beneath the apple tree carefully separating the dirt into one pile of fine sifted soil under the apple tree and another of rocks and pebbles next to the cesspool. At the time he had no use for either lot. He had been keeping busy and, of course, daydreaming. Now he had a use for the sifted fine dirt. He mixed it with water, making a fine mud, and plastered it around the base of the old tree. Day after day he applied each layer until he finally had a solid base over a foot high. After it dried he could stand on it and climb into his tire from it. At the end of the summer the solid platform would show hardly any wear.

One hot day Charles went to the store and bought a ten-cent water pistol. He returned home and started filling it in the pantry sink. His mother gave him a measured look as she watched him.

"You'd better keep away from the kitchen with that thing," she admonished.

Charles left, dribbling water from it as he inserted the rubber plug in the back. It was a bright green plastic automatic pistol, transparent enough to see what the water level was by looking through it.

He wandered down the street until he found Merle. Merle was deflating the asphalt bubbles melted from the pavement by the hot sun, using a sharp stick. The edge of the macadam was lined with collapsed black craters that had been systematically deflated. Charles promptly shot him in the back with the water pistol. Merle looked up surprised and shouted:

"Hey, wait until I get mine!" Merle disappeared into his house and five minutes later arrived with an identical water pistol of a different color.

A water war ensued until both pistols ran dry. The combat shifted to the hose at Merle's house. Harry showed up then disappeared home to get his water pistol. Mary Anne wandered by with her little sister in tow. They were both skipping a rope. Her sister was dressed in a white sailor suit with blue striping and stars in the corner flap on the shoulders. Merle promptly sprayed the little girl and Mary Anne headed home screaming at Merle that he would hear from her mother very shortly. The battle moved into the street in front of Merle's house. A hose was left dribbling on the driveway. Harry arrived with a big water pistol shaped like a miniature Thompson submachine gun. Adam materialized from nowhere with his weapon.

A mob of screaming spraying children moved around the street spraying anybody or anything that moved. It was punctuated by the addition of the nearby Baker Street gang kids. Everything that moved, including automobiles and some things that didn't move, got sprayed. There was a standing line at the water hose. Finally, Merle's mother got tired of the noise and came out ordering them to move on. The dripping wet mob drifted down the street to Harry's house where nobody could complain because his parents were at work. The melee lasted until all of the children were drenched from head to toe. Adam's dog Rex wandered by and was attacked by a dozen children. He retreated in a hurry with his tail between his legs while being pursued in force. Finally, the boys grew tired and were running out of things to drown. The group broke up with the soaking wet children going home to explain to their parents why it was not really their fault they were drenched.

Early the next day Merle arrived at Charlie's front door with a big bag of marbles.

"Let's play," he announced with a big smile.

Charles only had a few in a little net bag left from his last purchase. Merle left with Charles for the store to buy a replacement supply. Merle also wanted to buy a sheet of large square gunpowder caps for his blue finned metal bomb. He had been tossing it up in the air all morning to hear it detonate with a big bang when it hit the street. The store was closed. "Darn," Charles exclaimed, "I forgot the store was closed for the Fourth of July."

They went to the backyard and dug a small hole in the firm parched soil. Merle smoothed and patted the ground down around the hole. For an hour they played with the limited supply of marbles on hand. Eventually Merle won the few marbles that Charles started with. He could pitch them straighter than Charles. Somehow Charles had trouble, overshooting the hole by pitching too energetically. Finally, Charles was down to his favorite big red-swirled aggie. He pitched it against Merle's aggie and lost. There was a tear in Charles' eye as he saw Merle study the large milk-white and red glass marble. He looked up and saw the sad look Charles was giving him.

"Here," he said as he gave the marble back to Charles, "You owe me another big one. I don't want to take your last marble."

Charles was all smiles as he took the bright glass from his playmate. He knew he had a real friend with Merle.

They went over to Merle's house. Merle had a garter snake he had captured on his lawn one morning. It was a large, green, and thin snake about two feet long. Merle had boarded up a section next to his back porch and placed window screen wire over the top. He took a brick off the screen and lifted the snake out. Charles gingerly handled the snake. It wrapped itself around his arm and started moving up to his sleeve. Charles quickly gave the snake back.

"Gosh, it's fast. What do you feed it?" he asked.

"I feed it a hamburger. Raw hamburger is all it'll eat." Merle grinned as he concluded, "I call it the Hamburger Snake. It's a hamburger snake."

Later when Charles went home Rose asked him if he wanted to go to the fireworks show that night at the beach.

"Can Merle go with us?" he asked. His mother agreed but warned him that they had to go by bus. Charles ran outside and informed Merle that he could go to the fireworks with them if he wanted. Merle raced home to tell his mother.

When Charles returned to the house his mother confronted him.

"You know Charlie, I really shouldn't let you go after what I heard about your great fishing expedition."

Charles' face flushed as he tried to find a way out of the dilemma without disclosing what he knew.

"Oh, I didn't know anything was wrong," he innocently professed.

"Well, a little fairy told me you and the boys were at the Catholic church where there's a fishpond. Now, you wouldn't be telling me a lie, would you?"

Charles was speechless as his mind raced between finding an answer to his mother and trying to figure out how she found out.

"I didn't know there was anything wrong with going there. Honest," he lied.

"If I ever hear of you going back I'll let your father know and he'll punish you. Do you understand?" Rose knew that he would be checking with the other boys shortly to find out who gave the secret away. They would never find out that a neighbor saw them leaving the woods next to the church. It was easy to piece it together afterward.

"I'll never go back. I promise and hope to die if I do."

That evening after several bus changes they stood at the beach wall. The air was cool as it came off the ocean. At the designated time a shower of sparks sprayed from a barge far out in the bay. A thud sounded a few seconds later as the first rocket burst high in the sky. Charles and Merle watched in fascination as the magnificent display continued for almost an hour. A crashing finale filled the whole sky with color and noise ending the show. With a flash a single rocket rose and exploded to conclude the display. The following silence was profound. The boys walked along the beach behind Rose and Tom. Gradually the crowd dissipated until only their group was left on the deserted beach.

"Time to go home now, kids," Tom announced as they headed for the bus stop. The celebration was over.

That night Charles went to bed later than usual after the fireworks and a long ride home. He had fallen asleep in the last bus and woke up in Tom's arms while he was being carried into the house. He slept very soundly that night. In the deepest part of his sleep he had a profound dream. He was in a dense forest with another boy. The trees were very large and tall. They were walking together through the wild and mountainous terrain. The other boy was much taller than Charles and carried a rifle. A sudden violent storm caught them by surprise. The trees howled and bent with wind and rain. They were going down a winding path when both of them slipped on the claylike ground. The ground sloped to a cliff. They could not stop sliding and both of them fell off into space. Charles woke up in terror. He ran into his mother's room and crawled into bed with her. She put her arm around him and they went to sleep together.

Later that week the Marsh Street gang was in the clubhouse loft over the garage at Harry's house. It was hot and sultry in the early afternoon. The mischievous children were putting their minds together to find something to do. Four minds are better than one. Usually. They started discussing trivia for lack of something better to do.

"Why does your old man still wear a straw hat instead of a felt hat like everybody else?" Adam asked Charles.

"C'mon. He wears a straw hat because where he comes from, in Canada, everybody still wears straw hats," Charles responded defensively. "Why does your mother wear a veil over her face when she goes out?" he asked in return.

"She only wears a veil when she goes to church. She says it's fashionable," Adam responded.

"If you're an Indian," Harry was asking Merle, "Why don't you live on a reservation?"

"We live here because the white men, like your parents, took all our land and we had to do white man's work to survive. At least that's what my mother and father told me," he stated defiantly.

"If your old man is a lawyer," Merle was challenging Harry, "he is keeping the bad people out of jail."

"My father just defends the good guys," Harry responded.

It was Adam's turn again.

"Why does your old man smoke rotten cigars?" His question was directed at Charles.

"Those are good cigars, he only smokes White Owls." Charles responded, knowing what everybody but his old man knew, that cigars were rotten things—especially after they had been chewed on and the butt had gotten soggy. He had seen them around the house with teethmarks embedded in the brown wet mass.

The boys started laughing at the lie.

"Gee, I have a terrific idea," Charles said, eager to break the dialogue that would eventually end in a fight. "Let's get some cigarettes and practice smoking like our parents." Charles had always wanted to find out what it was like to smoke. If big people could do it, there must be nothing wrong, even if it involved matches and fire which everybody knew were dangerous. "Can anybody get any cigarettes from their house?" he asked.

The other boys suddenly looked interested. One by one they responded that there was no way to get cigarettes from home. They could not get them from the store either because of their age. Adam proposed a solution.

"Let's pick up cigarette butts from the curb on Main Street." Thus, it was agreed that they would scrounge whatever they could find from the gutter. They divided into groups of two and started out for Main Street. As Charles neared his house he invited Merle in for a minute.

"What in the heck are you doing?" Merle asked as Charles rummaged through his tobacco box of change and old Indian head pennies and V nickels.

"I've got an idea. I'm going to buy the corncob pipe that the store has for sale. It's only ten cents. We can put tobacco in it."

Charles suppressed a grin as he asked the grocer for the yellow corncob pipe for his father. The grocer gave him a cynical look as he took the pipe from the cardboard display. 'He can't do any harm with a pipe,' he thought. 'It's perfectly legal to sell it as long as it isn't liquor or tobacco.' He handed the pipe over and Charles paid him.

On the way out, Charles was grinning from ear to ear. Merle was waiting outside. Charles handed the pipe to Merle who looked at it quickly and gave it back. They started picking up cigarette butts off the ground being careful to look around each time to be sure nobody was watching them.

Later on, the boys reassembled in the loft. On the table, which had been retired from service in Harry's house, lay a great assortment of cigarette butts. Adam had hit the cigarette butt jackpot at the bus stop. They began segregating them by brand. A few with lipstick were discarded. There were also a few cigars. Adam stripped down some of the Old Gold pile and stuffed them into the pipe. Harry lit the pipe and they started passing it around like a peace pipe, with everybody taking small puffs from it. After the first round Merle commented that nobody was inhaling the smoke.

"You're all sissies. You aren't supposed to taste the smoke. You're supposed to breathe it like this." Merle took a deep demonstration breath through the pipe and promptly began coughing. With a red face he handed the pipe over to the next boy.

For two hours the pipe passed around and around the circle. The piles of cigarettes began to disappear. First the Old Golds, then the Chesterfields, and Camels, then Lucky Strikes, the Philip Morris, and finally the Pall Malls. Smoke filled the room with some of it escaping through the open window in a steady stream as if the garage was on fire. The boys were all coughing and looking a bit pale. Finally, the only thing left on the table were two short brown cigar butts complete with teeth marks. Charles looked at Adam who gave him a nod. He peeled the wrapper leaf off and threw it in the tin can that held all the white cigarette wrappers, lipstick cigarettes, and the grey ash from the pipe which now showed some blackened wear and tear around the bowl. Then he loaded the pipe with the bulk of the first cigar after being careful to pinch off the black and the chewed ends.

The pipe made the rounds again. Loft air changed from grey to blue. The second cigar was operated on like the first. Finally, it was ingested with the previous lot.

"I don't feel good," Harry groaned as he started down the stairs in a hurry to get outside to the fresh air. The other boys followed, coughing and rubbing smarting eyes as they stumbled down the stairs. After they got outside Merle looked up saying, "The place looks like it's on fire." He was referring to the column of smoke coming out the window.

Adam leaned on the side of the garage and started throwing up. The group slowly departed for home. Charles reached his house when a wave of nausea overtook him. He threw up on the lawn. June saw him as he staggered to the house and ran out to help him. At first, she felt sorry for him until she smelled his breath. She helped him inside muttering,

"You're going to catch the Devil from Dad for smoking." Then she saw Rose and announced, "Charlie's sick as a dog!"

Rose saw them coming and after helping him inside, realized the root of his problem. His clothing, hair and breath stank of cigarette smoke.

"You look like the wreck of the Hesperus, Charlie," she exclaimed while leading him to the bathroom where he threw up again. His face was white. "This will teach you not to smoke," she said as she watched his agony. Then she gave him a tablespoonful of cod-liver oil to settle his stomach and get rid of some of the cigarette smell. His father would be coming home soon and she didn't want him to know why he was sick—at least until the boy was well enough for further punishment. After his stomach had settled down, she put him to bed. Charles did not say his prayers that evening even though he was sure he would need them like never before.

Chapter Eight

Muskrats

One very hot summer day Charles boarded the bus with Rose and June, carrying blankets, towels, and a lunch basket with them. Charles also held a pail and square-ended tin shovel. They were going to the beach. After several changes of buses, they arrived to join the hoard of people trying to escape the heat like themselves. There was a water fountain on the walkway at the seawall where Charles and his sister took a long drink after a short wait in line.

Rose and June shook out the blankets and lay down to get the suntan they had come for. June started talking about the Fourth of July evening she spent with her latest boyfriend. They had gone to the town park to watch the bonfire ceremony and the large fountain brightly lit with colored lights.

"They had to put a guard on the log stack because someone tried to burn it down the week before," June commented.

Charles moved closer to the water and started digging a sandcastle. The tide was coming in so he worked at the outside edge where the sand was damp. Furiously he dug a large circular hole while placing the sand uniformly around the sides. An hour later the hole was a foot deep and five feet across. The walls were a foot high and very solid with a rounded top. Water had crept into the bottom of the hole. The water helped compact the sand as he smoothed the tightly packed walls. Gradually the tide came closer and closer until it licked around the fort.

Charles worked harder knowing that time was limited before the walls would be swept away. He piled sand on top while the waves grew bigger and closer, eroding more of the wall away each time.

Suddenly Charles felt a sharp pain as he reached into the hole for more sand. He looked at his finger as blood poured from it. Using his shovel, he dug up the cause of his problem. A four-inch purple-shelled razor clam had been residing in the sand until he disturbed it. He put it in his pail and resumed digging and patching his disintegrating fortress. A wave washed over the front of the fort. When it subsided, there was still water around the outside. Now water began to seep through the base of the walls themselves. Water also began to rise inside.

Charles sat back to wait for the eventual destruction of the fort. Finally, a large wave rolled over the weakened front wall filling the hole. Charles walked back to the blankets. His mother and sister were lying on the blankets with their eyes closed. They did not see him coming. He took the razor clam out of his bucket and gently dropped it on his sister's belly button. She sat upright suddenly and screamed in surprise from the cold wet clam. With a surprised look she gingerly picked it off her pink skin. She inspected it while giving Charles a rotten look. Then she threw the clam at him hitting him on the leg. She went back to her suntan.

Charles, grinning like a fool, limped away to the water. The slope of the beach was very gradual. Charles walked into the water until it was up to his armpits. He saw a stick of wood floating out quite a way. 'Can I get it?' he asked himself as he kept walking slowly into the small waves and increasing depth. He took smaller steps when the water reached over his shoulders and the waves had an unsettling effect on his ability to move. The stick was still out of reach. Very slowly Charles kept moving towards it. A wave splashed into his eyes and almost rocked him off his feet. He felt light and buoyant. He knew he had to make one last move forward in a hurry to get the stick or he would be swept away with the next wave. He took a deep breath and moved forward on his tiptoes. His eyes were under water. He reached out and touched the stick. He was almost floating in the water.

Charles could hardly control his movements. A thought flashed before his mind that he needed to do something extra to get the stick and get back to the beach. He thought of the metric clock. He was into the forty minutes of his time. In his mind he was a super person and could finish anything he started. He grasped the stick and started to walk backwards. He could not swim and had no intention of learning this way. Holding the stick over his head he backed off until the water level had receded and he could catch his breath again. Then he turned around and half floated, half walked back to the beach until he had control of his movements again. As he opened his eyes a stranger came up to him and asked him if he was in trouble. "No trouble," he answered. "I'm okay."

After he was back at the blanket he laid down and contemplated what he had done. The thought that he could have drowned did not occur to him until that moment.

On the bus heading home at the end of the day he asked himself again why he had done it. The answer was that he had not considered the danger of getting the stick from the deep water. The only thought that had occurred to him was whether or not he could get the stick. He smiled when he realized that he had transformed the metric clock into a powerful aid to help him when he was on his own. There was, within him, an ability to escape from the present to accomplish things that he could not ordinarily do. And although he had been in a dangerous situation he had not felt any fear.

That evening he woke to a pounding noise in the bathroom. After a few minutes it subsided and he drifted back to sleep. When he came downstairs in the morning June led him outside. A large dead muskrat lay on the porch. It was brown, furry, and about a foot long not including the tail.

"Dad caught it in the bathroom last night and beat it to death with the toilet plunger!" June explained. "Look at the size of the thing!"

"Wow!" Charles exclaimed as he poked at it with his shoe. "That was a really fat rat. It sure is dead now."

Rose came outside and hustled them in for breakfast.

"When you're finished, Charles, I want you to get a shovel and bury that thing in the yard," she ordered.

Later that morning there was an official burial with all of the neighborhood kids in attendance. Even the Baker Street gang heard of it and arrived to witness the laying away of a great rat. Charles gingerly picked the rat up by the tail and dropped it into the hole that the kids had dug next to the cesspool for the occasion. The word went out that giant rats were loose. That evening every family was discussing the news around the dinner table. The Main Street Market sold out of rat-traps the next day causing the grocer to make a special trip to the hardware supplier to satisfy the immediate demand from his customers. Within a week everybody had rattraps hidden in places where only a rat would dare to go.

A week passed. No more rats showed up at the house. Tom did not bother to buy any traps. He always had his plunger with the broomstick handle if the rats got in his way. The excitement died.

It had not rained for a month. Everything was drying up. Everything except Tom's garden. Almost every day Charles would pull up bright red rhubarb stalks for his mother's pies. She would twist the green leafy tops off and chop the stalks into small cubes to be cooked with much sugar to take out the sourness. Charles was watering one morning a week after the rat incident when Adam came running into the yard. His face was red from excitement.

"Quick! You have to come with me!" he demanded. "Come see the rats!"

Charles turned the hose off following Adam down the street running as fast as he could. Adam did not stop until he reached his backyard. A wooden box was against the back fence where Adam would survey neighboring yards for changes and especially to torment the dog in the yard behind him. This time there was something different. Adam pointed to the clothesline near the house that was fenced off from the dog.

On the clothesline were five muskrats all pinned to the line with clothespins over their tails. The heads were all smashed and bloody. Small beady eyes and whiskers protruded from where the traps had smashed a wire bar across the heads as they fed. A woman opened the back door and started sweeping the rear porch with a straw broom. She saw the boys and smiled at them. Then she went inside and closed the door. Because she had no children her husband would have to eventually bury the rats. But not before at least fifty children had paid Adam a penny each to stand on his box and review the gallows.

A few days later Merle showed up at Charles' house while Charles was riding on the tire swing. He proudly produced a fat and heavy red shotgun shell.

"Gee, where did you get it?" Charles asked knowing how precious an item like that was.

"I got it from Margaret on Baker Street. She found it in her attic. I had to trade my pack of Old Maid cards for it. Let's take it apart and see what's inside," he said anxiously.

Together they went into the cellar. Charles rarely went into the cellar of the house unless he had good cause. This was his father's domain. Half of the cellar was reserved for the furnace, the coal bin and the 55-gallon drum of oil for the stove. The other half was his father's workshop. There were tools all over the place, hanging from the walls and piled on shelves and the workbench itself. A huge cast-iron engine lathe occupied one corner. Wide leather belts that once turned its wooden wheels showed age cracks and much wear. Tom had collected it from a firm that replaced it with newer equipment. It had been run once after installation, making a great deal of noise when all of the belts were moving, but not afterward when Rose complained that there was really no use for it at the house.

Charles cleared a place at the workbench. Merle held the shell down while Charles proceeded to operate on the end of it with a screwdriver. The waxed folds were readily pried open and lead balls about a quarter-inch in diameter rolled out.

"Gee, that must be buckshot," Merle exclaimed. "I can use them for my slingshot."

They counted eight pellets and placed them in a small tin can that previously served as a cigar ashtray. Prying the padding from below the shot was a harder task because it was well-sealed and helped waterproof the powder. After substituting a pointed awl for the screwdriver, they were able to pick the padding out. They poured the grey powder into another container.

"Let's go someplace and burn it," Charles suggested intending that it be anywhere but his house or yard. He still remembered what happened to him the time his father caught him lighting a fire next to the apple tree.

They ended up at Merle's yard. Behind a tree that blocked the view from the house, Merle applied a match to the powder and watched it disappear in a flash.

"Wow! That was great!" Merle exclaimed. He ran into his house and came back with his slingshot. The slingshot was made of oak wood, filed painstakingly by a coarse bastard file and hand-carved by Merle himself, with a wide strip of automobile tire inner tube stretched across it. He held it horizontally and placed a lead ball on the rubber. Then he grasped it between his right thumb and forefinger and looked for a target. His first shot was the board fence dividing the backyard. It hit a board with a loud thump. Charles retrieved the ball from the grass and reported the size of the dent it made in the board.

Taking turns, they shot at the fence and, at one point, at a cat that made the mistake of being curious and walking along the two-by-four support near the top of the side fence. They both missed one turn each at the poor unsuspecting cat. Both misses went over the fence to be lost in the yard next door. The cat moved on unaware that its life had been spared.

"Darn, why don't we let the Hamburger Snake loose and shoot at it?" Charles suggested as the cat disappeared.

"Naw, the snake is dead. It curled up like a corkscrew and stopped eating. My dad said that the snake didn't get enough vitamins from eating hamburger all the time."

Finally, all the lead balls were lost and the game was over for the day. There was only one thing left to do.

Charles stood back as Merle knocked at the front door of Margaret's house. A little red-headed girl in a blue-flowered dress came to the door.

"Hi. Can we talk to you for a minute?" Merle asked as he stepped away from the door.

Margaret looked back into the house, then came out closing the door behind her.

"What do you kids want?" she said curtly. She knew it had something to do with the heavy red thing that she had traded with Merle that morning.

"Can you get me any more of the round red things that you gave me this morning?" Merle asked. He tried to hide his anxiety. The shotgun shells were definitely forbidden property for any child. He did not want to frighten the girl.

"That was the only one in the attic," she responded. She knew there were more of them but sensed that she would get in trouble if anybody found out she was taking them. Besides, she reasoned, they could be valuable or important and she did not know what they were. If her parents should miss them she would really be paddled.

Merle asked her to look further in case she had missed some of them in the attic. He and Charles left despondently. A great day was ending as quietly as it had started.

"I have an idea," Charles said as his face lit up. He was reluctant to let the rest of the day go by with nothing else to do. "Let's get a package of peas and a peashooter. We can shoot the street up with it without hurting anything." He was thinking about what would have happened if they had hit the cat with one of those lead balls.

They raided Merle's kitchen cupboard and found a half-full box of dried peas used in making pea soup. Charles had a yellow plastic peashooter hidden in the grape arbor outside his house. Rose had taken it away from him the last time he used it when he zapped his sister on the leg. He had accidentally discovered it in a cupboard and rehidden it for a day like today.

Together they went up and down the street taking turns at bouncing the hard peas off everything in sight. Nothing was spared as they shot up fences, mailboxes, trees, and a few windows when small children looked out to see what the noise was. They ended up at Merle's house again. The cat had returned and was comfortably lying on the top board of the fence. The warm summer heat had left it half-asleep, half-awake in a state of mind to think about past great days or nights on the prowl. It had not been scared away because none of the lead shots had got close to it from the slingshot. The big grey tomcat had many hard years of fighting experience and scars for proof. Patches of fur were missing from its coarse hide and the ears were torn and ragged. The tomcat's tail was crooked from a chance encounter with a kitchen door and an unkind housewife during a foraging expedition. The cat was tough and seasoned. He also had a powerful voice to match. The tomcat had been spared the deadly slingshot to experience the next worst thing that could happen to it. By now Merle and Charles very good at hitting targets with the peashooter. They were getting to the end of the pea box and were looking for a worthwhile target. The cat was all they could find.

Merle had the peashooter in his hand when they discovered the cat. It was both his turn and his cat. He searched through the pea box for a proper projectile. He rolled a large proper-sized pea in his fingers and inserted it into the tube. Then he took a deep breath and blew it through the tube as hard as he could. The pea hit the cat on the head. The pea was silent but the cat was not. It screeched at the top of its lungs. Then it ran along the fence and disappeared before a second shot could be dispatched.

The back door opened. Merle's mother heard the cat screech and ran out to investigate. She stood on the back porch with her hands on her hips looking at the two grinning kids with the peashooter in hand.

"Merle!" she yelled, "Come in the house this instant!" Merle's face changed from elation to despair as his mother advanced and grabbed him by the back of his shirt collar. She marched him into the house as Charles retreated. When he got home he was grinning again, remembering how loud the cat screeched when it was hit by complete surprise. He stopped grinning later that evening when Rose got off the telephone with Merle's mother and told Tom how Charles had wasted their peas.

Chapter Nine

Excursion to the Marsh

The August heat wore on. Finally, after a drought lasting over a month, thundershowers arrived drenching the community with dark clouds, great amounts of water, and lingering humidity. The lightning was exciting to watch and listen to. A long series of thunderstorms marched across the little town (only days apart) for several weeks. The change excited the children. They would huddle in the clubhouse with the candlelit waiting for the next clap of thunder to follow the lightning as it branched across the sky. The clubhouse window would rattle as the wind threw rain at it. Sometimes the lightning would be close enough to light up the clubhouse and the children would wait in awed silence for the deafening thunder to follow. They started counting out loud to measure the distance from the flash to the noise. This evolved into a game to see who could guess the correct number that would bring the crash. Harry suggested that the numbers could be seconds and warned them about counting too fast. If any of the boys were scared they gave no indication of a lack of courage. They were all very brave in a collective situation. 'There is truly strength in numbers,' Charles thought, as they huddled together one stormy afternoon. The eyes and expressions of the children were otherwise, however, when a storm was especially violent.

At one meeting the gang agreed to sneak out at night to catch nightcrawlers. It was agreed that they would all meet at the clubhouse in the rain after dark. Charles was caught by Rose as he was sneaking out of the house with Tom's flashlight. She returned him to the comfort of the living room for the remainder of the evening.

The next day Charles visited Adam to find out how the event went.

"Nobody showed up." Adam stated adamantly. "I was here all alone in the dark, smashing them." He started grinning as he pointed out the squashed remains of dead nightcrawlers littering the yard.

"What a mess! What did you smash them with?" Charles asked as he surveyed the pogrom.

"I used my baseball bat." Adam proudly announced as he produced a baseball bat with nightcrawler pulp encrusted over the rounded end. He walked over to his little brother's sandbox and started grinding the end of the bat in the sand to clean it off.

"That's horrible," Charles cried with a sheepish grin. "What will your little brother say when he finds out?"

"I won't tell him if you don't," he replied with an evil grin. "Besides, sometimes the cat goes in there too." Then he went back inside his house to go somewhere with his mother that morning.

That morning after the storm had passed, the air was left heavy and sultry. Water still ran down the streets and the leaves on the trees hung heavy and dripping. Rose asked June and Charles to go into the hills and pick some blueberries for dinner.

"I can't," June declared, abhorring the thought of spending the afternoon doing such a menial chore. "I have a date with John this afternoon. We're going to the beach and he's going to take me on the rides."

Charles knew what she was up to. Whenever she had a boyfriend with any money she was sure to find a place to help him spend it. She was going to get the most out of life while she could. Being popular and getting away from the house were her major goals in life. She was expected to get a job when she graduated from school to help pay her way at home. There was no possibility of going to college even if she could get a scholarship. The only way out was to get married. Her grades were all at the top of the class. Being accepted by the National Honor Society would be no problem. The problem was what to do with it.

"Well then, you'll have to go alone, Charles," his mother said. She let June off without an argument because she knew it would be futile to argue with her and that Charles would not object to going. He would rather go with his sister but they had little in common because of the years between them. Charles liked being alone at times and the trip to the hills would do him some good. She knew the reason he was still home in the middle of the day was because the neighborhood kids were unavailable and Charles would be hanging around the house if she didn't find something for him to do.

"That's not fair. I don't want to go," Charles said to protest his sister's escape from the chore. "I don't see why I should have to go alone."

"Are you afraid that a grizzly bear will eat you?" June taunted. She was looking for a reason to get revenge on her little brother for some of the things he did to torture her. Just the week before, she had been sleeping late after a date the night before. Charles snuck into her room and saw her foot sticking out from the blankets. He promptly painted her big toe with her good nail polish. Suddenly she woke up and discovered what he had done, chasing him down the stairs into the kitchen with a shoe in hand. He was saved from the beating by hiding behind Rose and hanging on to her skirts.

Charles looked at his sister a moment before going into the kitchen to accept his defeat gracefully. He knew when he could not win. He did not really object to going into the hills. He just liked company when he went away from home. His sister was smart and always doing things. He liked being with her or to get her attention. Rose came into the kitchen and made Charles a lunch of several peanut butter and jelly sandwiches wrapped in wax paper. She also filled a quart glass bottle with water and put ice in it. She gave him a quart Mason Jar for the blueberries. "Be careful not to fall and break the bottles or hurt yourself." she warned as Charles headed out the door.

"I'll be okay," Charles said without looking back.

Charles headed to the main street. He had a good long walk ahead of him. He angled across the street and started up the hill where the stream crossed under the road. The stream coursed in a zigzag fashion over granite bedrock. Not much grew along the stream because of a lack of soil. The water was very clear and he stopped to take a long drink. Then he continued his climb.

After climbing to the top of the waterfall hill he saw what he wanted. There was a valley directly behind the hill and on the opposite side was a larger hill covered with small scrubby blueberry bushes. He walked to the bottom of the hill and crossed a stream before starting up the other side. The sun was getting hot with vapor rising from the wet ground. Charles started sweating from the exertion and humidity. He was very uncomfortable.

He climbed halfway up the hill and followed a narrow path to some blueberry bushes. He put his bottles and lunch on the path and proceeded to pick the berries. The blueberries were small and hard. They had a light grey coating on them that brushed off to show the true dark blue as he pulled them from the bushes. The bushes were only a foot high and he had to sit down to get close. He proceeded to pick away as the sun rose higher in the sky. After a very long time he had filled the jar to the top. He had been tempted to pick some of the large blackberries that filled large bushes along the path. They would have made short work of the afternoon, he thought. The lunch had been eaten and the ice water long gone. Mosquito bites caused his arms and legs to itch. The sleeves of his short sleeve shirt were brown from wiping sweat from his face all afternoon. It was finally time to go home.

He took a different route back. Instead of going over the waterfall hill he decided to go around it. He headed away from the meadow and school direction following the stream in the valley between the hills. He carried only the blueberry jar now with the lid firmly snapped in place. The water bottle had disappeared in a splash of splinters when he tossed it at a big rock. A dirt road crossed the valley. Charles noted the location for future exploration.

As he rounded the side of the waterfall hill he saw a chicken lying in his path. The chicken was obviously dead. Some of its feathers were on the path next to it. Maybe a dog killed it, Charles thought as he stopped to inspect it. Whatever killed it was not hungry enough to eat it. Maybe Adam's dog Rex did it. He envisioned a fight between the big shaggy dog and the chicken with feathers flying all over the place as the chicken tried to escape with its life. Charles picked the chicken up by a leg. Flies buzzed away in anger from being disturbed. Maybe Mother can cook the chicken for dinner, Charles thought as he inspected it further. The chicken did not appear to have anything wrong with it other than being dead. Charles picked it up by both legs and headed home with the blueberry jar in one hand and the chicken in the other.

After a long walk he burst through the back door of his house and proudly announced to his mother that he had brought home something better than blueberries. She had been working with the washing machine in the pantry. It was crowded in the tiny room after rolling the washing machine up to the sink. She was wringing some clothes through the double rubber rollers with some of the hot water pouring into the sink. Looking up she saw Charles holding the blueberry bottle in one hand and the dead chicken in the other. She wiped the sweat off her face with her apron and went over to see what he brought home.

What she saw made her get even hotter.

"Get that rotten chicken out of here!" she yelled. "Go outside and bury that thing in the yard! Why did you bring that thing home? It's rotten and stinking."

Charles' face turned from joy to gloom. He had made a mistake. How could he have known that the chicken was no good. He went out to the cesspool area and dug a hole just big enough to hide the chicken. As he dropped the chicken into the hole he discovered maggots crawling out of the rear end. He hastily covered the hole and tried to forget what he had done.

That evening Rose told Tom that Charles had brought a rotten chicken home with the blueberries and Tom laughed so loud that Charles left the table abruptly with a red face. Tears were in his eyes. June did not easily let him forget his mistake when she heard. It was a full week before Charles was not reminded of the rotten chicken he had brought home for dinner.

That weekend Tom noticed a strong repugnant smell in the backyard. He found the cesspool overflowing into the soil around it.

"Rose," he said, when he went into the house later in the day, "there's a prime stink in the yard. The cesspool is overflowing. You need to fetch the honey wagon and have 'em pump it out. It's been years since we had it cleaned so I reckon it must be time again."

Charles was in the kitchen at the time and overheard the conversation. He started for the back door to see what he had missed.

"Charles," his mother cried, "keep away from that horrible cesspool!"

Later that day he contemplated what the honey wagon would do when they came. Charles was looking forward to the operation, which he hadn't witnessed before. On the following Wednesday he was waiting on the front porch when the horses pulling the long round tank arrived. An older stout man went up to the front door leaving a younger and thinner man holding the reins. The tank was about ten feet long, in the bed of a wagon pulled by two very hardy horses. The tank was painted with very pretty shiny red paint and the words "Honey Wagon" in bright yellow on both sides. In smaller letters on the sides of the wagon was "Jones Cesspool & Plumbing Service." The older man returned and walked into the yard while motioning for the wagon to follow. The wagon was halted beside the cesspool. They tied the horses up to the apple tree. The horses promptly started eating the wormy apples which had prematurely fallen to the ground.

The men got out a large steel rod with a hook on the end and pried the cast-iron lid off the cesspool. It fell to the side of the mound with a thud. Then they got out a large hose and inserted the end into the stinking mass. Charles wandered over to look into the cesspool.

"Keep out of the way, kid!" the younger man yelled. Charles backed off. The other end of the hose led into a pump located in the back of the wagon. The older man started cranking furiously with the long handle that projected from the pump. Gradually he slowed down and started to pump slower and steadier. A gurgling noise flowed through the hose and into the tank from the other end of the pump. The waste material made a splash inside the hollow tank.

Charles watched for a few minutes then ran down the street to tell his friends. Harry was the only one he could locate. The thought of a cesspool being pumped out did not induce Harry to leave his house. Charles went back home again. The backyard stank from the open cesspool. The men had changed places while the pump handle was still going up and down. Charles watched the man's muscles flex and sweat stand out on his forehead as he steadily worked away. The steel tank sounded less and less hollow as the black sewer fluids and solids kept pouring in. Rose came to the back door and saw Charles watching the men.

"Get in the house this minute," she ordered, not wanting him around the smell and getting in the men's way. Reluctantly Charles retreated to the house after taking one last look at the workers.

The next morning Harry, Charles, and Merle were gathered in the clubhouse. Vacation was half over and the gang had not planned anything together.

"Darn, before we know it," Merle was saying, "the summer will be over and we'll be back in school wishing we had done something with our vacation."

"What do you suggest?" Harry asked, looking at Merle and then at Adam and Charles.

"I think we should go fishing." Charles suggested, "but not for giant goldfish."

Adam and Merle broke out in a grin. "I don't know a good place to go fishing," Adam said, "but we could go to the marsh."

Charles looked worried. He had started to go to the marsh alone before but had gotten scared and returned home. It was a long hike. None of the gang had been there before. Charles had heard stories about the marsh from other older kids. It was supposed to be a dangerous area with rivers of water running through it, poisonous snakes, and muskrats everyplace.

"The marsh is a scary place," Charles stated. "Nobody goes there except murderers or escaped convicts. Gosh, do you think it would be safe if we went together? It would be a horrible place to get lost or drowned." His face lit up, "I'll go if the whole gang goes."

Adam and Charles looked to Harry and Merle for an answer. Two for and nobody against the idea yet. Merle nodded an okay then everybody waited for Harry's approval. Harry was conservative in everything he did. His mother had always warned him not to take chances or do things without her approval. That's why he had turned down the fishing trip and realized that he had been correct in doing so. He missed the fun but kept out of trouble and that was more important. A trip to the marsh was not as much trouble as trespassing. He knew that the fishing trip was wrong before they started. A trip to the marsh could be put down as a normal day with the kids. He also knew that if he kept declining things with the boys they would not ask him to be one of them even though he owned the clubhouse. He I nodded his reluctant approval.

Early the next day the four boys and Adam's dog Rex started out for the marsh. There were two ways to get there. One way was to follow the street they lived on and continue into the grassland where it ended. The other route would follow the waterfall stream from where it went under Main Street until it ended up in the marsh. They decided to walk down their street into the marsh and follow the stream out. That way they would be covering different territory each way. Along the way Adam raided a bush in a front yard and ripped off a branch which became his switch. He switched at everything in sight, including the rear portion of his dog when it got too close.

"Hey, get away from me with that stick. You're dangerous," Harry warned, as Adam switched and slashing everything around them.

At the end of the street a vast grassland began. It was the edge of a saltwater marsh that stretched inland for many miles. It was forbidden territory. The boys walked through tall grass until it thinned out. Then they were able to see a dirt road to their right that led deep into the marsh. They cut across to the road.

They followed the road for a mile to where it ended at a large rock. The rock stood out in the middle of the marsh. It was the only thing higher than the grass. It was the town shooting gallery. Everybody in town went there to shoot their guns. The rock served as a backstop and a place to stand cans or bottles. The open marsh would absorb any shots that missed. The boys were elated with their discovery.

"Wow! Look at the shells!" Merle exclaimed, as he ran to the rock and picked up empty shotgun shells that littered the end of the road. He stuffed them in his pockets until they were full.

"Watch out for the glass," Harry warned as Adam climbed over the big rock.

"Look, I found some bullets!" Adam yelled, picking up some smashed lead forms from the rock crevices and resting places where the bullets had been trapped. He kicked a pile of glass and broken clay discs off a flat spot on the rock. In a few minutes he had a handful of metal slugs and fragments.

Meanwhile Charles and Harry were picking up shotgun shells and brass cartridges from the ground. There was a fascinating array of different items to be collected. It was not long before the boys had their pockets full of treasures to carry home.

The sun was directly overhead with the heat being felt by all the boys.

"I'm thirsty," Adam stated as he climbed off the rock and recovered his switch. "Where do we go from here?"

"We can get a drink from the stream on the way back if we go the right way," Charles suggested. "Why not go further into the marsh and head towards the stream when we turn around?" The road ended at the rock and there were no paths to follow into the marsh. They were on their own now.

They went deeper into the marsh. The ground continued to slope gently in a plane leading to the sea. Their new course headed at an angle which took them in a straight line to the street where they began. They knew the trip home would be harder than the hike there because they would be tired. After walking for a considerable distance, there was a change in the ground underfoot, which turned wet and spongy. The air also was different. It smelled like rotten vegetables.

Suddenly they were looking at the edge of a long broad channel which had been filled with salt water at high tide. Now, at low tide it was a deep cut in the marsh with a black stinking muddy bottom that sloped to a small stream coursing down the center.

"Wow," Merle said. "Look at that creek. It really stinks here." He looked at the other boys while waiting for their comments.

Harry was quick to respond, "Let's get out of here. This place is dangerous."

By now he and the other boys were lined up on the side of the grassy plain looking down into the forbidding channel. Suddenly Merle saw something move along the water's edge.

"Hey, I see something!" he exclaimed as he leaned over the edge to get a better look. "Maybe it's a muskrat." He leaned further over to see directly below and suddenly slid over the edge with a surprised yell. He fell down five feet landing sideways in the black muck at the edge of the channel. The boys watched in horror as he landed. The dog started barking furiously as he stood near the edge and saw the boy wallowing in the mud. Merle stood up and surveyed his position with a look of disgust on his face. He was knee deep in more than a foot of mud. His entire left side was dripping with the slimy mud from his abrupt landing.

"Help get me out of here!" he cried in desperation. The other boys had been too shocked to move. Slowly Harry lay down on the grass.

"Grab my feet, Adam, so I won't fall in," Harry directed as he inched forward until his upper torso hung over the side of the chasm. He grabbed Merle's outstretched hands. By digging his elbows into the grass, he was able to inch backwards with Adam pulling one leg and Charles pulling the other. Merle got close enough to the top to reach out for another hand.

"Boy, do you stink!" Charles commented as Merle's muddy form slithered over the top. He grabbed Merle's hand and pulled him over the edge until he lay prone on the grass.

With his tail stuck between his legs Rex cautiously sniffed the slime on the boy's clothes. The boys lay on the grass not saying anything for a minute as they surveyed the gravity of their situation.

"We're lucky that Merle didn't drown or get stuck in the mud," Charles said. "Let's get out of here."

The suggestion was equal to a consensus. The boys started the long hike home. Adam resumed switching at the grass and weeds again. After a long walk they found where the waterfall creek ran into the marsh. It washed into the same saltwater channel that Merle had fallen into. They followed the water through brush and a large stand of cat-o-nine-tails where it entered the marsh. A clear section of creek opened up where the creek flowed over a sandy place. The boys sat down to drink the clear water and take a rest. Merle wallowed in it afterward to wash the mud off his clothes. The water turned dirty brown.

They resumed their march. Adam made a better switch from the stalk of a big cat-o-nine-tails plant. Dragonflies buzzed overhead as they walked along dense growth near the creek. They came on a small pond formed by the creek. Tadpoles were swimming about in it. Charles tried to catch some with his hands but was only successful in getting wet. They continued on. The marsh had changed to a light forest of small trees and brush.

Adam switched something in a tree and suddenly a swarm of bees was after him. He raced ahead trying to beat off the swarm that surrounded him. He started screaming. There was nothing the other boys could do. They stared in horror as Adam tried to outrun the bees. Rex followed with his tail between his legs yelping and barking furiously. The children ran in all directions to keep away from the bees swarming around the smashed hive in a furious attempt to protect their home.

The boys arrived home separately. They were out of breath, scared, and very exhausted. Charles worried about Adam. After dinner he went by Adam's house. As he approached he heard the dog howling in pain. Adam rocked back and forth in a rocking chair on the front porch crying. His face and arms were covered with salve his mother had applied. The exposed skin was red and swollen from multiple bee stings. The dog lay next to him. His long black nose was bumpy and swollen from bee stings. Charles asked if he was okay and if there was anything he could do for him. Adam did not answer and kept on crying. Charles went home feeling terrible.

That evening Charles lay in bed thinking about the bees chasing Adam and the dog. He wished he could have invoked his metric clock to help save him in some way. He went to sleep thinking about the swarm of bees, his friends, and the dog.

The next day Charles found Adam again rocking on the porch and sobbing without tears from the pain.

Chapter Ten

The Harvest

*S*ummer evenings grew shorter. The sun would set before Charles could get away from dinner after his father came home from work. Cool night air replaced the heat of the long hot summer. Soon school would start and summer freedom would be gone. The children in the gang felt an urgency to do more with the little time left.

Tom was eating dinner with the family. He was in a very good mood this particular evening.

"What are you doing tomorrow, Little Charlie?"

Tomorrow was Saturday and Charles had made no plans. Saturday was his movie day but he was not looking forward to a double feature of musicals this week. It was unusual for his father to call him Little Charlie. Something was afoot. "I don't have any plans," he paused to see what the reaction was and added cautiously, "yet."

"I'm thinkin' it's time to harvest the string beans. I'll let you sell some, the part we don't need, 'n you can keep some of the money for helping me plant 'n water 'em. What do you think of that?" Tom grinned at Charles, knowing he could not turn the deal down.

"Gosh, I think it's a great idea," Charles responded. He did not know how much money he could earn but he was excited at the prospect of keeping busy for the weekend. The family had been picking and eating string beans for weeks and if they didn't sell off the remaining crop it would go to waste. Charles hated string beans. Rose would snap the top off and strip the thread running down the seam in the center, cooking them in a dozen different ways, but they always tasted tough and wirey.

"Next week, Little Charlie, you 'n I are going to visit one of my brothers in Canada for a few days. It's been a considerable few years since I've seen him. That'll give you something to talk about when school starts up again." The family rarely went anyplace because they did not have a car or the desire to spend hard-earned money on things they did not need. But Tom had decided it was time to visit the farm where he had grown up and see relatives he had not seen in many years and Rose agreed. It would give Charles a chance to see other people and places.

Charles was bright-eyed with excitement. He was finally going on a trip. There would also be some money in his pocket from the bean crop. He went over and hugged the big man in a rare show of emotion. Tom smiled and put his arm around the small boy that he knew so little about.

The next day Charles was up bright and early pulling the hard string beans off the vines. He made sure he did it correctly so a small stem was left on the bean. He worked all morning with Tom until they had ten-bushel baskets full. When they finished Tom lugged all of the beans into the cellar where they would keep cool. The sticks were pulled from the ground and also stored in the cellar. The vines were left on the ground to replenish the soil for the next year. Tom dug out an old rusty spring scale from one of the corners where things were piled about. Then he made a wire basket out of twisted coat hangers and hung the scale from a nail in a ceiling beam. He gave Charles a quarter.

"Git to the market on the main street. Buy as many reg'lar two 'n five pound bags as the grocer will sell you. We'll need 'em for the beans."

Charles rushed to the store. At first the grocer was reluctant to sell store supplies to the boy.

"What do you need them for, sonny boy?"

"Please, my father and I picked a big load of string beans from our garden and we need bags to sell them," Charles responded. He was annoyed at the grocer slowing him down because he had so much to do. He didn't want to keep his father waiting.

"Well, if that's what you need them for I can help you. You won't get more than a nickel a pound for the beans at this time 'cause most people just don't like them. I don't even carry them at the store. If I did I wouldn't sell the bags 'cause you would sell them to my customers and I'd have to throw mine away if I didn't sell them." He went into the back room and came out with fifty bags and fifteen cents change for the quarter Charles had given him.

Charles ran home and met his father in the cellar. They had more than enough beans to fill all the bags. They worked together filling and weighing the bags. Tom was careful to put some extra beans in each bag so the weight could not possibly come up short. Charles told him what the grocer had said about pricing them. Charles brought his old red Radio Flyer wagon to the cellar door. Together they filled it with the bags of beans.

"Get ten cents for the small bags 'n twenty cents for the big ones, they aren't worth more'n that," his father advised as Charles started down the street pulling the wagon.

Rose ran to the front door.

"Take this change purse, Charles, so you won't lose the money." He stopped and doubled back to accept a small flowered cloth snap purse.

Finally, he was on his way with half of the bags in the wagon. It was noon but he had not bothered to stop for lunch. He didn't want anything to slow down his task for the day. Slowly he went up and down his street. Some people were not home. Others did not like string beans. About one in ten people bought one of his bags. Most of his load was sold locally so he returned home to fill his wagon with the remaining bags. Then he repeated the routine he used to sell seeds. He went into a strange neighborhood that was farther from home. Fewer people were now interested because they did not know him. One person offered him nine cents for a bag.

"It doesn't look full," she said. He sold it knowing he would have trouble selling all of the beans.

All afternoon he went door to door hawking the beans. Very few people were interested in the large bags. Some people bought the small bags just to be nice. 'A person really has to like these tough string beans to buy a big bag full,' Charles thought to himself as he analyzed the results. Finally, all of the small bags were gone. Only five of the big bags had sold leaving him with twenty left over. He wanted to sell them all that afternoon because the next day was Sunday and he knew that Rose would not let him bother people. Suddenly the tired and hungry boy noticed the strong smell of food cooking at the last few houses he visited. Charles decided to reduce the price in order to sell them before it got dark. He marked his price down to fifteen cents and sold a few more. One lady seemed more interested when he told her he had just reduced the price. After that he raised the price back to twenty cents and told everybody that the price had been reduced from twenty-five cents to twenty cents so he could go home early. It was easy to sell the big bags after that. By the time it was dark Charles had sold his beans and was trotting home pulling the empty red wagon.

Charles ran into the house. He had missed the dinner hour but his mother had saved some food for him. He was too excited to think about eating. He took the change purse out of his pocket and dumped the contents on the table. Tom came into the room and the three of them counted it out. There was $7.39 in the pile.

"Charles did a great job today," Tom said very loudly so that his sister upstairs behind locked doors would hear. "I think you should get half of what you sold for luggin' that wagon all over town." Then he took four dollars off the table and gave it to Rose. "You can buy Charles some fancy new clothes with this money."

The rest of the money was in change which Charles put into little piles of common denomination so he could count it again. Then he went upstairs and brought down his flat Prince Albert pipe tobacco box of coins and his savings. He dumped this on the table and counted out almost ten dollars total savings. Finally, he shoved it into the tin box and went to look for his dinner on the stove.

The next day Charles walked to church with Mary Anne. He had not seen much of her since school had closed in June, as she had been away most of the time with relatives in the country. She gave him a piece of maple sugar candy shaped like a pine tree that she had saved for him in New Hampshire. Charles nibbled on it slowly letting it melt in his mouth because he had never tasted anything so good.

On occasion Charles had gone to the movies with her and walked her to church several other times. When she was home between trips she would play with her girlfriends and babysit her little sister.

"I miss the days when we used to go to school together," Charles said as he remembered the daily walk and how they would always have things saved up to talk about. He had liked the routine. Now Mary Anne seemed a little taller and skinnier than before. She also did not appear as close to him as she used to.

"Gosh, I've been awful busy this summer. I missed seeing you while I was away. This fall we'll be going to back to school together. We can be close friends again." Looking at Charles as she talked she noticed that he seemed a bit more talkative and outgoing than she remembered him. 'The summer has kept him busy,' she thought. 'He's probably not as bored as when he was in school all day long.' He was still the same height as her and just as skinny. Today he looked as small as ever with short brown pants and a red short-sleeved shirt tucked in the elastic waist. She felt something changed from before. They had been apart so much that when they went somewhere together now they were almost like strangers. She had seen him playing with the boys many times but could not spend any time with him because she would be with the other girls or with her little sister in hand. She wondered how he felt about her now.

"I was really worried about you when I found out that Adam got stung by the bees. You must learn to be more careful." Mary Anne's mother had heard about the trip to the marsh from Adam's mother. Her mother had used it as a lesson on the dangers the children could get into. Mary Anne knew boys were always getting into trouble. They were not like girls. She liked hearing about the things the neighborhood boys did. It was more fun to hear what happened than to actually be there. That was about as close to trouble as she wanted to get.

"Adam made a mistake. He was darn lucky though because the doctor told his mother that he could have died from all those stings. Even Rex got stung on the nose. Life is dangerous sometimes and a kid needs to be lucky to stay alive." Charles was holding Mary Anne's hand. He gripped it tighter. The trip to the marsh had been a really wild day. He knew that if the tide had been up Merle might have drowned when he fell in the channel. Sometimes he got scared by the things he did or things that happened with the gang. But he was never scared until the danger was over.

"Did you miss me?" Mary Anne asked softly as she swatted a mosquito that had attached itself to her dimpled knee. She was wearing a short yellow dress with straps that came over a white blouse with ruffles on the collar and short sleeves.

Charles looked at the little girl. 'I wonder if she will look like her mother when she gets big,' he thought. 'I imagine that she will have to become a teenager like my sister first. That would be horrible. I hope that she stays like she is now. I like her this way—ordinary and uncomplicated, like me.' He gripped her hand and looked shyly down at the sidewalk. "Sure, I always miss you. Sometimes I'm busy having fun with the gang but when I'm alone I think of you. Charles slowed down to kick a rock and added:

"I'm going on a long trip to Canada with my father next week. We have relatives there and he's taking a vacation from work to visit them. I've never been away on a trip before. I'll miss you." He got excited as he talked about the trip. His mother had bought him new clothes during the week. He thought they were for school but now he knew that they were also for the trip.

"You'll like going away," Mary Anne said thoughtfully. She always got bored in a hurry after she was home a few days from visiting relatives. She did not have as much to do as the boys on the street when they got together.

They parted at her church. Charles went on to his church and did not hear a word that was spoken. His mind was on the Canadian trip. Later that day he bothered his mother and father endlessly with questions about where they were going and what they would do when they got there.

That evening his mother packed a large suitcase for Tom and a small one for Charles. Almost all of Charles' new clothes went into his little suitcase.

Later Charles lay in bed bathed in excitement over the trip the next day. He did not fall asleep until early in the morning.

Fall

Chapter Eleven

The Journey

Tom woke Charles early. Charles was groggy from not sleeping well the night before. Rose made a quick breakfast and held them both tightly in her arms before they left. June was still in bed. Only an earthquake or fire could move her at this hour of the morning. It was still dark when they left for the bus stop with suitcases in hand. The early September morning was cold and the darkness made it seem even colder. As they waited for the first bus the sun began to rise over the horizon. At first only a glow was noticeable. Gradually the shadows of night became the sharp forms of day as the edge of the sky turned orange and then golden yellow. When they boarded the bus, Charles asked Tom if they could sit in the back. After they were seated Charles continued to watch the sunrise through the back window.

"What do you think of the sunrise?" Tom asked, seeing Charles' fascination with it.

"Gosh, I love it. It's great. I don't remember ever seeing a sunrise before. It's really beautiful," Charles answered as he observed the top edge of the golden globe rise above the trees and houses in the distance.

"I see it every day on my way to work. It be one of the things that I look forward to. Many days I also see the sunset on my way home. Look around you at the people on the bus. They're cold 'n many of 'em have bad jobs that are very hard and pay very little money." he stopped to look at the passengers, all men, bundled up in overcoats, scarves, and wearing felt hats. Dark colors, mainly greys and dark browns, dominated. "Yes, indeed, when a person has to work very hard he finds little things to look forward to. I always sit in

97

the back of the bus whenever I can so I can watch the sunrise or sunset. We're going West now 'n when we come back we'll be going East. This puts the sun behind the bus both ways. I go to work the same way. It makes the long rides worthwhile except when it rains or snows. Of course, I appreciate the good weather after a fearful storm. I reckon that's what makes life worth living." Tom paused and realized that Charles might not be absorbing his philosophy. After all, a philosophy must be both learned and lived to be appreciated. His coarse hard hand squeezed a fragile arm.

"We'll be taking an ocean ferry later on. I know you'll like it. It's ponderous' slow but very different. It's not fancy but we'll make do because it's all we can afford.

The morning wore on with other bus changes and a ride in a subway train. The fast-electric train was packed with rude and harried commuters. Charles stood up with his father, clinging to his hand as his father held on to a strap hanging down from a bar bolted to the roof. Charles worried that if he ever got separated from his father on the train he would never be able to find his way home. The train swayed and lurched noisily from stop to stop where people surged on and off. Eventually they got off with one of the waves of disembarkers. They walked up a set of stairs and found themselves in a huge terminal where buses stopped and parked at one side and trains stopped at the other.

They walked past the trains to a gate at the end of the building. A man sold them tickets from a window in a small office. Another man in uniform was stationed near a gate where people began to line up. Charles sat on his suitcase in the line. After an endless period of time Tom disappeared for a few minutes and returned with several hot dogs and French-fried potatoes in his hands. He was rewarded with a big smile.

"I hope you're hungry because I fetched this for your lunch 'n it'll have to last all day," he said, handing Charles his portion.

Charles slowly ate the rubbery hot dog and warm French fries. Afterward he felt much better and the tired feeling that accompanied him all morning went away. Then it was his father's turn to stand with the luggage while Charles went off to the restroom. The wait resumed.

Later, when Charles was convinced that the line would never move and that everybody would go back home, a bag of pretzels appeared from Tom's pocket.

"Here Charles, have some. They're made with fish oil the way good pretzels should be made."

Charles took a handful and found them delicious.

Suddenly there was noise and movement at the head of the line, which started to shuffle forward. When they arrived at the gate Tom gave the tickets to the man on the left while a man in a different uniform with a gun at his side looked the passengers over from the right.

The line filed out onto a dock and the people walked directly up a ramp into a ship deck. The ship appeared huge and awesome to Charles who had only seen them in pictures. A white-uniformed captain stood at the end of the ramp greeting the passengers as they boarded. The ship emitted loud complaining noises as it ground bobbing up and down against the dock, from choppy seas due to a storm far out of sight in the vastness of the ocean.

Charles and Tom boarded and walked along the deck that divided the cabins from the iron railing at the edge of the ship. They found a pair of lounge chairs against the cabin wall and settled down with a view of the dock and flow of passengers.

"Make yourself comfortable, Charles. We're going to be on this thing until tomorrow morning. The cabins were filled 'n there weren't no way to get us a cabin for the night. We'll spend it deckside where this almighty cold weather will keep us company." He didn't tell Charles that there wasn't enough money to rent a cabin for the night. He knew it would be cold at sea but there was no harm in the boy learning to live with a little hardship before he grew up. It would keep him from getting soft and helpless like a woman.

After a long wait, a whistle on the ship blew loudly, then the ramp was pulled up and the hawsers let go from the huge dockside posts. Sailors, in dungarees, watched the thick ropes snake across the deck and wind around two motorized capstans. The ship's engines started running strongly with thumping noises deep in the bowels causing a vibration at the deck underfoot. Tom grinned and turned to Charles:

"This ship sure isn't a proper luxury liner, like the Queen Mary."

Slowly the ship turned away from the dock as it headed out to sea. The buildings receded into the distance as the old ship thumped into a choppy unfriendly sea. A windy afternoon passed slowly with Charles exploring every inch of the ship he could get into. The size and solid steel plate construction with rows of rivets holding it together fascinated him. He found it hard to believe that a ship made this way could be watertight.

Charles, who had never seen a full sunset, watched the sun setting. Usually the sun hid behind hills or trees but tonight it was in full view and sliding into the edge of the ocean. The color changed from gold to orange then deep blood red as it slowly receded over the horizon. A sky full of clouds was painted by the colored rays until they became black with shadow and oncoming darkness. The air suddenly became chilly and inhospitable. A cold wind came from nowhere washing over the iron ship with the small boy at the rail.

Charles was quiet as he absorbed all the new events and surroundings. His father had been unusually quiet smoking his White Owl cigar in contemplation of the homecoming. Sometimes the smoke would swirl annoyingly around Charles as he sat next to him. A steward in a white uniform came by and informed Tom that it was the last call for dinner. Tom thanked him and nodded to Charles to follow.

They went into a big dining room that filled the top end of the ship from side to side. It was comfortably warm. They were seated at a large table covered with a white linen tablecloth with linen napkins and silver-plated silverware in front of them.

"This is surely more fancy than the oilcloth your mother has on the kitchen table," Tom commented as he saw Charles looking around in awe of the surroundings. "You can order anything you like tonight, Charles, it'll be a long night 'n I want you to be happy. I figger whatever you order will be better than that chicken you brought home. I bet you expected your mother to cook it for you with feathers 'n all." Tom slapped his leg and laughed to himself at Charles' expense.

Ignoring his father's humor, a flushed and starved Charles looked at the menu without understanding anything on it. The only thing he recognized were the oysters. He had eaten fried clams before at the beach stands so he reasoned that oysters could not be bad. After all, they both grew in shells. When the white-uniformed waiter arrived for the order Tom ordered a steak and Charles ordered oysters.

"Those be oysters on the half-shell, Charles," his father commented. "Are you sure that's what you want?" Charles nodded and the waiter left.

A half-hour later the waiter arrived with the food. Charles took one look at the oysters in the shell and turned white. They did not appear to be cooked. He looked up at his father. Tom looked at them, smiled, and with his country wisdom, commented, "well, Charles, it looks like they fetched what you ordered."

"I didn't know what they were. Honest, I thought they were like clams," Charles clammered as he stabbed one of them with his fork. The dirty grey jelly on the clamshell quivered in response. He looked up at his father who seemed to be enjoying his dilemma. "Let me trade my oysters for some of your steak?" the frustrated child asked, knowing he might starve to death if he could not satisfy his hungry stomach.

Tom nodded and they traded. Tom ate the oysters by spearing them with a fork, then his half of the steak. Charles felt his stomach lurch as he watched Tom lift the impaled jiggling oysters in the air. They had to be the worst thing in the world to eat. 'Maybe people who are tough enough to smoke cigars are tough enough not to care what they eat either,' he thought.

When the dinner was finished they found a set of chairs not exposed to the weather, inside a hallway next to the purser's office. Tom promptly went to sleep leaving Charles too excited to sleep in the strange place. He started exploring the ship again. Much of it was now chained off or locked up, limiting his travels. At the stern a sailor had thrown a log overboard. The log, which showed the speed of the ship in knots, was attached by a line to a gage bolted to the railing. The indicator pointed to seven knots as Charles watched. A phosphorescence trailed behind the ship glowing in the near darkness. The decks were clear of people, who had retired from the cold decks, to their cabins.

Charles moved to the railing at the front of the ship. The only sounds were the ship's engines and slapping water noises as the prow cut into the waves. A pang of loneliness overtook him as he looked out into the darkness. Nothing was visible beyond the lights of the ship except isolated stars as points of light in a cloudy moonlit sky. A middle-aged woman came over, standing nearby looking out at the invisible black water. She wore a black woolen coat, with dark hair knotted on top her hatless head resting in a heavy red-colored scarf. She looked sideways at Charles and smiled knowingly. Charles looked at her out of the corner of his eye warily.

"Aren't you cold young man?" the woman asked as she stood next to him.

"A little bit I guess," Charles answered as he looked at her and tried to respond to the stranger. 'It's nice to have company,' he thought. 'The rest of the people on the ship have all left and gone to sleep inside the ship someplace.'

The woman put her hand over Charles' on the cold metal railing.

"Oh my!" she exclaimed. "Your hands are cold." She looked at him softly as his mother would. Charles felt the warmth of her hand through his cold skin. He now welcomed her warmth and companionship. She looked directly at him as her expression changed to concern.

"Young man," she spoke slowly as if digesting the thoughts, she was translating into words. "You must get some sleep and be rested. Soon you'll be called on to find your strength and become a man." Her eyes were deep and serious. "Have a good trip and God be with you." She squeezed his hand firmly and gave him a broad smile as she left. Charles watched her melt away into the darkness as mysteriously as she arrived. He wondered what she meant about him becoming a man. He felt lonely again.

The night wore on but Charles couldn't sleep. The air gradually grew colder as clouds blotted out the entire sky. A light rain fell, quickly graduating to a downpour, drowning out the ship noise as it lashed against the passageway. Charles wandered back to look at the log again but could not find it in the choppy sea. He looked out into the darkness feeling tired and then migrated back to the chair next to Tom to sleep a fitful sleep. When he woke up to the cold rain the next day he felt as if he had not slept at all.

Chapter Twelve

The Mountain Farm

Tom and Charles watched the ship pull slowly into port to dock. Tom was chewing on a piece of dulse. He offered a piece of the dark leathery material to Charles, who bit off a piece and gave the rest of it back. Charles chewed on it for a minute and spit it out.

"It's too salty," he said as he looked up to see his father chewing and grinning.

Time dragged as the ship was finally tied up and they walked through Customs with their baggage. They stopped for breakfast at a counter, changed some currency, and boarded a train. The train was comfortable and Tom made sure that Charles found a window seat. As the train pulled out of the station Charles fell asleep. Tom watched Charles snoring in the corner next to the window, thinking, 'I wonder how this little boy will turn out when he grows up? He sure resembles his Mother's side of the family.' Then his thoughts flowed back from the present to fragments of the family he deserted so many years before. 'I wonder if they will be wantin' to see me after all this time? Maybe it's a mistake to take Charles this far if we're not really welcome.' As the train passed through a dark forest of pines Tom looked out the window and realized how homesick he was for the wild country and the people who lived with its gifts of beauty and nature.

Charles felt something poking him in the ribs. He looked up at his father.

"Wake up, Charles. We're here," he was saying with a big grin. Tom was standing in the aisle with their two bags on the floor.

Charles panicked and jumped quickly to his feet. They got off the train and Charles waited while his father had a bill changed and made a telephone call. They went outside and sat down on a bench.

The weather was starting to clear, but it was still cold. Charles knew it was colder than when they left home. It seemed weeks ago that he was going door to door selling beans. Now, just two days later, he was in another world and climate. The train station was at a dirt road at the bottom of a mountain. Large trees covered the mountain, unlike the small ones in the wood near Charles' house. The ocean bordered one side of the road. This road ran along the edge of the ocean bisecting the mountain range and the shore. The train ran parallel to the road in many places.

"You'll like this part of the trip, Charles," Tom was saying. "Them hills are where I grew up. You like the woods and country. Your mother 'n I moved from the city to the country where we live because it's much nicer. Now we're going to a real farm, where I was born. My relatives still live there 'n we'll be staying with them 'til we leave."

Charles was quiet. The trip was overwhelming. He knew he would soon be surrounded by new people in a strange place.

"Gosh, I hope they like me," he finally said. He knew he would now see much of his father that he had never seen before. He felt good about that. Deep inside he wished the four boys from the gang were here to share the trip with him. Charles actually felt uncomfortable with his father because he would be sharing the whole trip with him and he knew so little about his life and ways outside of home.

A large flatbed truck pulled up at the station. A husky man in bib overalls bounced out and he and Tom started hugging and embracing each other while talking furiously. Tom's younger brother finally broke loose and came over to shake Charles' hand with a vice-like grip. Tom introduced his brother, Ralph, to Charles. The luggage was thrown in the back next to a large tool chest and they drove down the dusty road together. From the continuing conversation Charles gathered that Ralph and Tom had not seen each other for the many years since Tom had left the homestead as a young man. Charles also noticed that the brother talked just like his father.

A cloud of dust followed the truck along the road. The strong smell of the ocean permeated the air and enlightened the senses.

They drove for ten miles with the ocean to the right and the mountains on the left. The terrain was rugged, with few houses or buildings to be seen. When there was a structure it was usually on the mountain side of the road. The ocean was not like the ocean Charles knew, with level sand for sandcastles as far as the eye could see. This ocean had a bed of rocks and boulders right up to the mountain road. It was harsh and broken, not a playground for the civilized to relax on. It was the Nova Scotia that the Arcadians had to leave.

Finally the truck stopped at a large white farmhouse. This was home. When they got out of the truck Tom pointed to the house and told Charles:

"I were born at this here place. There weren't no doctors then, just a midwife. I grew up in this old house. I also went to a one room schoolhouse where they taught me to write with my right hand, even though I was left-handed."

Charles stood still for a minute trying to absorb what he was seeing. The house stood next to a large rapid stream that came out of the mountains and went under the road into the ocean. A pickup truck was parked in the yard with a wheel jacked up into the air. A very large garden grew behind the house. Plumes of cornsilk protruded from ears of corn on tall stalks. On the ocean side of the street sheds stood near large nets hung between poles. The silence was broken by a group of children from five to thirteen years old who came out of nowhere to loudly greet the company. Tom announced that they were to be nice to Charles and then left with his brother.

The rest of the day was filled with social amenities, such as the children quizzing Charles about where he lived, his school and what he did for fun. They were surprised that he did not work at a regular job after school so he told them that he was in charge of the garden in the backyard. Later they showed him around the farm. They led him to a barrel of herring bait in one of the sheds next to the road.

"Go on, smell it," the biggest boy directed.

Charles stuck his nose over the barrel and took a whiff of the fish stored in the saltwater stew. It was the most rotten thing he had ever smelled.

"Phew! It's rotten!" he exclaimed as he rushed outside for fresh air.

The big boy laughed and stuck out his hand for the first time.

"I'm Robert. That's a prime stink for you. We catch the herrin' in big nets 'n store 'em in barrels until they get good 'n ripe. Then we use 'em for bait in these here lobster traps. The lobsters love rotten herrin'." With a flourish he pointed to the ten-foot row of wooden lobster traps stacked in the open like cord wood. The boy stuck his fist in the opening of a lobster trap. "See," he said, "the lobster climbs in to get the herrin' 'n he can't get back out again."

Then he pointed out the two big boats that they rowed into the bay to set the traps and nets. A scream came from one of the children gathered near the fishing gear.

"Quit the yellin' 'n git out of here!" the boy admonished as the smaller children moved back to the house.

The boy continued the tour by taking Charles to the herring nets stretched out between poles stuck in piles of rocks.

"These nets are made from cotton 'n rot if we don't keep 'em dry. When we're fishin' we put the nets out so the herrin' will swim into 'em when they follow the tides and currents. The herrin' swim into the nets 'n get their heads stuck. They can't back out 'n get free 'cause the net closes behind their gills. We have to be quick to bring the nets in afterward or the big fish will eat 'em while they're stuck." The boy smiled as he saw that Charles was absorbing his lecture on fishing.

Then the mentor marched across the street to show Charles where the outhouse was and to point to the mountain.

"That mountain is the wildest one of 'em all. We shoot the biggest deer 'n sometimes a bear back in there," the older boy announced proudly. "That stream," he said, pointing to the wide and fast running stream near the house, "comes from the top of the mountain where there's a great lake. Whenever it rains the stream gets big 'n wild."

When it was dinner time the boys let Charles pump the water at the sink for the bucket. As he cranked the curved cast-iron handle up and down he noticed the pump was a smaller version of the one that the cesspool men used to pump the tank out. Charles was very happy to be in such a different and exciting place. Robert, his cousin was already a good friend. He knew he would have a good time.

Linda, the aunt, served dinner with homemade bread and fresh corn with butter that tasted better than anything Charles' mother ever cooked at home, well almost as good as baked beans, he thought.

The fresh butter and milk was from a big brown and white cow in the yard. Charles made up for his lack of appetite from the past few days.

After dinner a coveted bottle of Canadian Club whiskey appeared and the clink of the bottle touching glasses went on into the evening. Adult voices and laughter grew louder and more animated until the empty bottle was discarded.

Charles stayed outside watching the fireflies switch their tiny lights off and on in the darkness, which was filled with cricket and insect noises. Then he went to bed with his father and slept soundly for the first time that week.

When he woke up the next day it was almost noon. The only other person up was Ralph who was repairing the tire on the pickup truck. Later on Ralph disappeared with Tom to visit old friends and places. The children milled around Charles all day until their fathers' return. Charles followed them under the house to chase chickens off their nests and pick up brown eggs. At the end of the day there was a flurry of activity around the fishnets and sheds. One of the big rowboats was being readied for a fishing trip in the morning. Naturally Charles was eager to go along with them.

That evening Tom was in a very outgoing mood. Charles had never heard him talk so much. He was a changed person. He was truly a man on a much-needed vacation from his dawn-to-dusk routine at home. Another bottle of Canadian Club whiskey moved about the dinner table between the adults. Charles was glad to see his father so happy. He knew Tom had enjoyed many happy times on the farm as a boy. Charles intended to share that as much as possible while he was here.

It was dark and cold when they got up the next morning. By now Charles knew his way to the outhouse but found someone in it when he got there. Instead he wet a nearby tree and went in to wash up for breakfast. The kitchen was warm and comfortable from a wood fire in the stove when he returned. Shortly afterward they left for the boat. It was cold, foggy, and hard to see, even though the sun was rising. Voices drifted strangely through the mist from one person to another.

The boat was pushed off the rocks and they rowed out to sea. Fishermen, like all true seamen, have a fine sense of where they are at all times and what to do. These men were no exception and were able to arrive at the first of the lobster traps in the dense fog. They pulled in a brightly painted wooden float and the line attached to it. The trap was empty. The bait was also missing. Ralph put a handful of herring into it and lowered the big trap back into the water until it rested on the bottom of the bay again.

They moved on to the next float and pulled the trap in. It held a green two-pound lobster.

"This is a good one," Ralph said with a smile. "We have to throw back any lobsters under a pound so they can grow up 'n get caught again." The lobster went into a large box in the middle of the boat.

The next trap held a large lobster with only one claw.

"Look Charles, this one got in a big fight. I'll bet he lost it in a fight with another lobster," Ralph commented as he held it up for everyone to see. "This old boy's been around for years. Look how big he is. Even with only one claw he must weigh more'n five pounds." He had been talking for Charles' benefit because Tom knew what he was talking about.

By mid-morning the sun had dissolved the fog and they neared the end of the trap line. Noisy seagulls circled overhead. They were excited by the smell of the fish and the activity on the water. The nosey birds were always interested in whatever was happening on their ocean. Charles had taken over the job of bailing the bilge with a coffee can. A large codfish was taken out of one of the traps.

"That's our dinner tonight," Ralph commented as he pulled it out of the trap by its tail. A small shark also shared one of the traps. "Them dogfish tear up the nets 'n traps. They're the fisherman's enemy." Ralph commented as he took out his knife and sawed the little shark's head off before tossing it back into the water.

Finally the boat headed back to the shore with the box half full of lobsters and the fish. Everybody pulled the boat high up on the rocks near the road. It was a long pull because the tide had been going out since they started in the morning. Ralph and Tom took the lobsters away to the fishery in the pickup truck. Charles went into the house carrying the cod in both hands. He gave it to Linda, who thanked him with a big smile.

"Did you have a good time?" she asked as he watched her cut it apart in the sink.

"Gosh, today was one of the greatest days of my life," Charles replied enthusiastically. Linda was pleased that part of her routine and perhaps mundane life had proven to be a great experience to the child stranger.

Charles saw the water bucket was empty and started working the pump handle at the other sink to fill it. He liked life on the farm because there was a lot to do and it was interesting. His thoughts turned to speculate what it would be like to live there all the time. He could not imagine why his father left the good life on the farm to go to the city and suffer so much during the Depression.

Robert, the solidly-built lad of thirteen had taken a sincere liking to Charles.

"Can I take Charles to the boat to help clean it up?" he asked his mother.

"I don't see why not," she answered. She was glad to see Charles go off and keep from getting in the way. He was a nice boy but she did not like anybody getting underfoot and disturbing her routine.

They went to the boat and scooped out the bilge that had collected. The big box was removed. Unused bait was thrown out on the rocks. Seagulls circled overhead impatiently waiting for them to leave. "Phew, this water stinks," Charles commented as he was bailing out the dredges.

"Everything about the ocean smells strong," Robert responded. "When you've been around for a while you get used to it. I even like it. The herrin' in the barrel smell good to me." He grinned when he saw that Charles was having a hard time believing him.

The day stayed cold. After the fog lifted, thick dark clouds had drifted overhead. Robert decided to take Charles exploring the beach to see what flotsam was lying on the rocks for their inspection.

"During the war," Robert stated, "a Liberty ship was torpedoed off the coast by the Germans. All kinds of things were floating or dragged into the rocks by the current. There were life rafts, wooden boxes of medicine, even landmines were drifting in for a while." He had Charles' attention now. "We took the rifle and shot up the landmines. They made a fearful bang when they blew up. We're lucky none of them came near the bait shed or boats 'else they'd cost us dearly."

They walked along the beach picking up weathered pieces of wood and rusty metal. Robert mentioned that the salt water corroded everything but brass very quickly. Charles saw a large form laying on the rocks far ahead.

"What's that?" he asked, expecting Robert to have an answer for everything.

"Beats me. Let's take a look." Robert had not seen the shape before. Things were always arriving on the rocky beach and just as fast sometimes disappearing again.

When the smell reached them it was obvious what the form was.

"It's a big dead shark," Robert said as he started running to it. The shark had been a giant before it had died. Now it was a rotted mass of decomposing flesh deposited on a rocky beach. It was an imposing sight with a smell that overwhelmed Charles after a very short time.

"Phew! It stinks! Let's head back," Charles said as he turned around holding his nose and walked away from the source of the terrible smell.

Robert took a piece of driftwood and stabbed it.

"Look at it quiverin'," he gleefully shouted as the form moved. On the way back Robert asked Charles if he would like to go hunting with him the next day.

"Las' summer we got a big buck not far from the house. That was the best-tasting venison we ever had. For two whole weeks we had meat every day instead of fish." He knew Charles had never been hunting. Robert still needed to convince his father to let Charles go with him. Although he had been hunting before with his father, Ralph had never let him go alone.

"Gosh, I'd love to go," Charles said getting excited at the thought of going into the mountains with Robert, who knew everything about hunting and fishing, "What kind of gun are you going to take with you?"

"I thought I'd take my father's 30-30 lever action Winchester," Robert said matter-of-factly. "There ain't any better deer rifle."

Charles did not like the idea of anyone shooting a deer, especially after seeing the Bambi movie. He did want to go hunting, though. It might be okay if I just go along and don't have to hurt anything myself, he thought. Besides, we might not see anything.

That evening Robert received reluctant permission from his father.

"We've a dry summer 'n the deer are probably quite a bit back in the mountain," he advised Robert. "Get an early start 'n be prepared to do some walking."

Charles spent a restless night in anticipation of the big hunt the next day. After tossing and turning about for a long time, he fell off into a deep sleep.

Chapter Thirteen

The Hunt

*C*harles was up with the sun, after waking to a boisterous crowing rooster in the yard. Robert was still in his room sleeping so Charles left him alone and wandered through the house as the family got up. He filled the water bucket, his favorite chore, which always seemed to be empty. The water was slightly discolored.

"Why does the water look funny?" Charles asked his aunt, as he pulled the bucket out of the sink.

Linda came over and looked into the bucket.

"It'll settle out. We've had a fearful dry summer 'n the water level is very poor. 'Specially at this time of year. Likely you'll see a bit of sediment from the bottom of the well in the water." She lit the wood-burning stove and put the kettle on.

The kitchen had warmed when Robert came through.

"Ma, please pack a lunch for Charles and me?" he asked. Robert expected his mother to do things for him as she would for her husband. Ralph had let everybody know a woman's place was in the home, serving the men who were expected to work away from home. In this way there was equality of labor. Each person in the family had his or her place, with chores delegated by decree from Ralph or indirectly from Linda to the girls and smaller children. This division of labor worked quite well in the household.

Tom came in and promptly settled down at the kitchen table across from Charles.

"What do you think of this here simple country life?" he asked Charles.

"Gosh, I love it here. It's swell. I don't know why anybody would ever want to move or do anything different."

"This is the good life, Little Charlie. There be no alarm clocks, no busses to catch, no bosses to yell or complain, no neighbors talkin' about your silverware being worn or the dishes chipped." Tom held up a brassy fork that had once been silverplated. "Ralph 'n the boys catch some fish or lobsters, grow some food, or work at loggin' further down the mountain. You never hear tell of them complainin' or going hungry. I reckon there's everything a man needs here, where a body can worry more about the weather than his neighbors. We'd no need of them, but to help or trade things they have to much of, not to complain. A man's word and a handshake in these here parts is worth a hundred lawyers. In these parts a man needn't put things in writing. It's easy to be honest 'cause everybody knows everybody and strangers aren't welcome." Linda placed hot food in front of Tom and he stopped talking.

Linda had to say her piece.

"It's not really that easy, Charlie, even if your father makes it seem as easy as fallin' off a log. Sometimes the price of lobsters is bad, or there is only a little rain 'n the garden does poorly, or the children get sick 'n there's no money for a doctor, or the gov'ment shipyard stops buying lumber 'n there's no work in town. Sometimes it's easy as can be 'n other times I have to kick my husband out to find work or get busy." She set Ralph's place and, having served the men, sat down to eat.

Uncle Ralph entered the room and handed Robert the rifle. The bluing had rubbed off the barrel and the stock was scarred and scratched from many years of handling.

"I want you to be mighty careful," he said, knowing that Robert might be inclined to show off with Charles at hand. "Keep the safety on until you're ready to fire it. There be only three cartridges in it. They're expensive 'n I don't want you to waste 'em by shooting at anything not good for the dinner table. Likely you'll not see anything anyhow, so don't blow up any poor rabbits with this here rifle." Robert was a very serious boy for his age, but Ralph felt the warning was necessary because he had always been with the boy when they went hunting.

Robert proudly grasped the rifle. He and Charles went to the large building behind the house. Robert took a cotton rope off the bench inside.

"When we kill the deer we can tie it to a big stick 'n carry it a'tween us." he said as he took a large hunting knife off the same bench. "I'll gut it with this here knife. That'll make it easier to carry back. If I don't gut it right away the blood will make the meat go bad." He took his belt off and ran the tongue through a slot in the back of the knife holster and buckled it up again. Robert showed Charles a heavy pointed knife with a thick back.

"This knife used to be a file. My dad ground it down 'n made a knife so strong I reckon it'll never break." He stabbed the knife into the bench to show Charles how sharp it was. Then he gave the rope to Charles to carry along with the lunch bag. They did not need to carry water because of the streams coming off the mountain.

"That's a swell hunting knife you have. I have a knife too. I won it at a school contest." Charles said as he proudly displayed his little knife.

"I'll use your little knife and show you how to gut the deer after I shoot him. Do you want to lug the rifle?" Robert asked.

"No thanks." Charles answered. He was afraid of it. He had never fired a rifle and was not ready to start. He knew how dangerous they were. After all, he reasoned, they kill animals and people.

They started down the dirt road. Robert carried the rifle in his right hand. He was in a great mood. Today he would shoot a big buck with a large rack of horns grown over many years of hiding from the hunters. If his father didn't have enough money to get the head stuffed and mounted, he would cut the horns off and nail them to the wall in the hallway and use them for a hatrack. A gust of cold wind made him button up his jacket. He looked up and saw a darkening sky filling with a billowing cumulonimbus formation.

"It's getting fearful cold out, Charles. I figger it'll rain today. Hope it doesn't rain afore we get back." He started walking faster, knowing they had a long way to go.

"I hope not," Charles answered. He didn't look forward to a long hike through the forest in a cold rain. He looked at the ocean and noticed that, even though the tide was going far out, the waves appeared to be bigger than the day before.

They reached a wide field and started inland. Large mature oak trees lined the far edge of the field. Beyond the oaks a pine forest began. They went through the field and into the forest.

"Gosh, what big trees!" Charles exclaimed. "In New England, where I live, most of the trees are small and skinny. There are also walls of piled rocks all through the woods everywhere." Charles' mother had told him that in Colonial times the forests had been cut down and much of the land had been farmed. The farmers had used the rocks from their cleared fields to establish the boundaries between farms. Poor soil and neglect caused the abandonment of the farms over the years with the land being given back to nature. Young trees now competed for the cleared land.

The ground started rising and Charles found himself short of breath. They stopped climbing when they came near a small meadow that appeared through the trees as a hole in the forest. Robert put his finger to his lips to indicate silence. He slid the safety off the rifle with a small click. It was the only noise in the forest. They slowly walked forward with Robert in the lead. He stopped and looked intently for movement in the field. There was nothing there.

They sat down at the edge of the clearing. Charles was glad to take a break from walking up the slope.

"My father shot a deer in this here field once," Robert stated. "We'll have to go much farther up this mountain to get to the next field. I'm thinkin' we'll see something afore then." Robert knew that their best chance of killing a deer lay in finding one in a field. When he and his father encountered deer in the forest they usually jumped out of sight in the trees before they could get a shot off. He pushed the safety back on the rifle and slung it over his shoulder.

They continued their trip. The grade kept getting steeper and steeper. They were not following a path of any kind. The boys wound around rocks and trees, always on the alert for the elusive deer. Birds and squirrels were everywhere and quite noisy until the boys got close. Then the forest would be quiet with the noise always in the distance ahead or behind. As they moved through a pine grove there was a great fluttering of wings and motion as a large bird took to the sky ahead of them.

"Gosh, What was that?" Charles asked startled, as he shied back when he saw the huge form take to the air.

"That's a chickenhawk. A real big one. I'll bet he could pick a chicken or rabbit off the ground easy as could be for his lunch." Robert was glad to have seen something. The whole morning had been a waste of time with the forest so quiet and dead.

A light rain started to fall. Robert quickened the pace. He was feeling disappointed. It was late morning when they reached the other meadow. They advanced cautiously to the edge of the clearing and stopped. Another dry run, he thought. This is going to be a bad day. It was colder now and rain had started falling steadily.

"There's nothing here either. Let's eat lunch afore we move on," Robert said.

After eating, they started up again, this time walking at a right angle around the mountain. The terrain began to change. The gentle slope became rocky with small cliffs appearing from jagged outcrops of granite bedrock exposed to the weather. Visibility shortened as the rainfall increased. Robert drove onward, insistent on finding a deer for the day. Charles dutifully followed closely behind, rarely saying a word of complaint or comment. They stopped at a large stream. After drinking some of the swift cold water, they resumed walking along the bank farther inland.

"Maybe we'll find a deer that's stopped at the creek for a drink," Robert said hopefully. "We can walk along the bank. More'n likely they're close to the water because of the drought. Keep quiet in case we get close to one. Try 'n stay behind me."

They followed the bank. The creek bent around a corner. Amid a stand of white birch trees, Robert spotted a deer. It had been eating grass in the large spaces between the trees. The deer looked up and saw Robert at the same time. The buck had short horns with fuzz on them from its two-year age. With a spurt, the buck headed up the stream away from the boys. Hooves clattered and clashed on rocks as water splashed. Robert's heart pounded as he sighted the open vee rear sight on the front bead, right on the deer hindquarters. He pulled the trigger. Nothing happened. Robert looked at the rifle and realized that the safety was still on.

"Damn! damn! damn!" Robert yelled furiously as he started after the deer. With Charles following, he splashed up the stream after the deer. They ran until the creek cut through a steep canyon wall and the deer turned fleeing into the forest. The boys slowed, breathing heavily, and walked up the hill bisected by the stream. The hill was high with a steep grade. They were out of breath when they reached the top. Rain poured heavily on them through the trees. They sat under a tree at the top of a truncated rise.

They were in a large pine forest. A wind suddenly advanced with increased rain. The trees bowed as the storm descended on them. They sat huddled behind the tree on the leeward side of the storm. They were cold and fatigued. Neither boy had a word to say as they caught their breath. A gust of wind made a moaning noise as it wove among the pine trees around them.

Charles found the noise startling. The trees and noise seemed remotely familiar. A chill shook him from head to toe. A foreboding overtook Charles. An ominous dreadful feeling he had never known before now possessed every fiber of his being. 'There's something wrong with this place,' Charles thought.

"Let's go back!" he demanded of Robert. "I'm tired and want to go home."

"Okay," his cousin said readily. The hot stove in the kitchen was foremost in his mind. He was worn out and would appreciate the warm dry old farmhouse more than anything at this time. "At least we saw a deer 'n almost got him. Let's just look over the other side of this hill first to be sure our deer didn't circle around the hill to get back to the stream."

They got up and walked across the top of the hill, descending the other side. Charles felt very strange and uneasy as they followed a narrow animal path that wound around trees and bushes. The wind continued making intermittent low moaning noises as it passed through the pine forest above them. Suddenly, Robert slipped on the pathway. Traces of grey clay on the path had become treacherously wet from the rain. As he fell he grabbed Charles. They both slid down the path a few yards. The path abruptly turned at the edge of a cliff that ran along the stream bed. Charles grasped at a small bush which came up in his hand. They plummeted over the edge of the cliff. For a moment there was weightlessness. Robert let go of Charles as they hurtled through space. They were screaming as they landed on the rocks below. Then blinding engulfing pain and darkness.

Chapter Fourteen

Escape from the Wilderness

Charles woke up feeling dizzy. He tried to stand, falling down for his efforts. For a minute he lay in the rocks and water of the creek bed, then got up on his hands and knees like a dog. The dizziness slowly passed away. A terrible headache replaced vertigo. Charles stood up and saw blurred images of a large rock a few feet away. He stumbled and splashed over stones and water to the rock and sat down. His head hurt so badly that he leaned forward and put his face in his hands. The pain did not leave. When he lifted his head up, his hands were covered with blood. All he could think of was the pain in his head. Slowly he reached down into the water and, cupping it in his hands, washed some of the blood from his face. He tasted the blood as it ran down into his mouth.

Carefully he felt his face and head to find the source of the blood. It was coming from a large gash on his forehead. He felt the open skin that ran from the hairline to his brow. Blood was still streaming down his face. He now became aware of other bruises and cuts on his head and body. He reached into his pocket and pulled out a wet handkerchief. Slowly he twisted it wringing the water out and tied it around his head. The cloth turned red as the blood stopped flowing.

Suddenly he remembered Robert. He had not even thought of his cousin as he was checking his wounds. Charles felt guilty. He stood up and looked around. Robert was lying on the other side of the rock where Charles was sitting. Charles slowly staggered around and found him lying sideways on the rockpile at the edge of the stream. His right leg lay twisted and sticking out unnaturally in front of him. Robert looked pale and helpless. 'Is he dead?' Charles wondered as he looked at the lifeless and broken form. 'I hope not. It would be terrible for Ralph and Linda to find him dead. He was a nice kid and smart about country things. Maybe they would even blame me for what happened.'

Charles went over and sat down next to him. After a minute he picked Robert up by the shoulders and held him closely. Charles could hear his irregular and shallow breathing. Slowly and then uncontrollably, Charles started crying. He held on to Robert and rocked back and forth with him in his arms as he cried.

When the tears subsided, he looked up finding darkness had fallen. It was still raining. Wind noises issued from the primeval forest. Clouds covered over any moon that might have lit up the sky. The night was black as pitch. The boys were sitting on scattered rocks at the edge of the stream. The creek would have been higher but for the summer drought. Charles dragged Robert over to the bank at the side of the hill. It provided some shelter off the rocks from the wind.

Robert did not waken. Charles felt his head and noticed some large bumps. One was wet with blood. 'What if he dies?' Charles thought as he sat next to him with his back to the bank. 'That was too terrible to think about,' he resolved. Charles started crying again and did not stop for a long time afterward.

Charles woke up. He had fallen asleep while holding Robert next to him for warmth and shelter from the rain. They had spent the whole night side by side in a sitting position. The sun cut through the clouds on one side of the sky. Robert was still unconscious. Charles made sure that he was still breathing and left him on the bank. He saw the rifle lying in the stream. Charles picked it up and found the hammer had broken off when it hit a rock. He threw it back in the stream. He was shivering uncontrollably from the exposure to the rain and water. He knew Robert would die if he didn't get help soon. And he knew he could die too.

Charles realized that yelling for help would do no good this far back into the mountains. He looked around. If he ran for help, Robert might wake up and wander off someplace and he would never find him again. Robert could even fall in the creek and drown. If Charles wandered off for help, he might not be able to locate Robert afterward. The thought of leaving the creek and returning afterward bothered him. 'I don't want to have to come back here again, ever,' he thought. Charles picked Robert up and took several steps. He was not strong enough to carry him any farther and set him down again.

Panic washed over him. 'I'll never be able to get him over the hill, and the creek is too deep here where it goes through the canyon. If I carry him through the canyon, he will drown if I drop him. And the water in the creek is rising from the storm.' Charles sat down to try to think out a solution to the problem. His head was throbbing and interfered with his ability to concentrate. He had an idea. 'The only way out of here,' he thought, 'is to follow the creek to the ocean. All of the streams cross the road when they get to the ocean. If I can make it that far, there will certainly be help from the dirt road.'

'But how can I carry him when he is heavier than I am?' he pondered. He saw the knife handle sticking out below Robert's jacket. Then he found his solution. He took the knife and rushed down the stream as fast as he could travel. The water was up to his chest at one part as he waded with the current at his back. He got through the canyon to the birch stand where they saw the deer. At the stand he cut down two small trees by hacking and sawing away with the knife. He trimmed the branches and tops off until he had two small trunks about five inches thick at the bottom end and four inches thick at the other end. The sticks were about seven feet long. He dragged them back against the stream until he was back with Robert. Wading into the stream to the broken rifle, he picked it up and took the leather sling off. He threw the rifle back for the final time.

Charles remembered a cowboy and Indian movie he had once seen. The Indians moved their belongings by tying them to two tepee sticks that they hung to each side of their horses. The ends of the sticks dragged in the ground behind the horses, leaving a groove in the ground and a small trail of dust. Charles decided to tie Robert to the birch sticks and drag him out of the wilderness.

Charles attached the sling across the sticks about eighteen inches apart. He did this two feet from the end. Then he took Robert's belt off and did the same thing about three feet further down. The belt narrowed the sticks to fourteen inches where it was attached. Charles now had a stretcher. Charles took the rope and ran it through Robert's belt loops and also around both sides of the sticks. When he tightened it Robert was lying with his back on the sling, his waist attached to the sticks by the rope with his thighs resting on the belt.

Charles cut the remaining rope and tied Robert's legs to the sticks, which were about a foot apart at the end.

He suddenly felt very tired. Charles sat down for a few minutes and thought about what he was doing. He looked at Robert, whose face was ashen and skin cold to the touch. Charles felt like crying again. He took a deep breath and stood up. There was no time for indecision or turning back. 'I must go or we will die,' he thought. Charles then got under the widest end of the travail and backed into position until the sticks were over his shoulders. Robert's head was slightly lower than his. Charles checked to make sure that he was still breathing and then started down the stream. When he went through the deep gorge one leg of the travail rode upon a rock and almost pitched Robert over on one side. The water seemed much deeper than the day before. The rain was swelling the stream. At the shallow place where Charles had gotten his birch sticks, he stopped and checked the stretcher. Robert was still attached.

The short trip through the gorge was exhausting. Charles was now colder than before and had very little strength left. The water drew body heat from him as it rushed past. 'I don't know how I can ever make it out of here,' he thought. 'It will take a miracle to survive. Where can I ever get the strength to get to the ocean?' The cold water was numbing his legs as it coursed past his thighs. 'I need strength and time.' Then he remembered the woman on the boat. "You will need all of your strength to become a man," she had said. Now Charles knew what she had known. Charles knew that there was not much time to get to the ocean before the cold and broken bones would kill them. An idea came to him. He imagined the metric clock. It filled his whole mind with the hundred-minute face and the hands racing around it. He reached into the clock with his mind and took the forty minutes of special time to gain the unique power to accomplish his goal. He would forge ahead to the ocean with the strength that the extra time could give him. He opened his eyes and saw only the blur of the water and forest on both sides as he splashed down the torrent with a strength he never had before.

For hours he kept moving relentlessly downhill. With the water pushing him from behind and with the grade in his favor, he was able to make good time without stalling. Several times he had to slow down for deep or exceptionally rocky places in the stream. Sometimes he had to navigate around trees that lay across the stream.

Fortunately, the banks were not too high on one side or the other. The coldness of the water continued to sap his strength. He pushed on not noticing the rain had stopped. The effort made him an automaton with his legs marching forward even though the calves were tight and sore. The sticks dug into his shoulders and it took all of his strength to hold on and keep pulling them forward. His shoulders were numb. Charles gritted his teeth and sometimes even closed his eyes as the effort overcame him. Stoically he kept pushing ahead knowing that Robert would die soon if he could not get to help.

Charles stopped at a shallow place in the creek. He could not go on any farther. He pulled Robert from the creek into a small grassy area adjacent to the water. Charles set the sticks and Robert down next to him. His stomach hurt from hunger. His head still hurt from the wound. He untied the handkerchief from his forehead to wash it in the creek. As he leaned over the water he passed out.

He awoke to find himself lying half in the creek. Only the shallowness of the water saved him from drowning. He crawled over to Robert. Robert was breathing very slowly. He looked awful to Charles, who was hurting all over. He now felt sick to his stomach from the exertion. He was exhausted. A pair of crows started cawing to each other from deep in the pine forest. 'If I don't go on,' Charles thought, 'Robert will die and he will never be able to hear the sounds of the forest again. He thought of his mother and sister waiting at home for him. They will never see me again. I have to try.' Again, he called on his metric clock to give him the measure of strength to carry on.

Charles painfully picked up his travail and started down the stream. After a timeless trek down through the dark forest he found himself staring at his feet. He was paying attention only to where his next footstep was going. His concentration was so intense that he had not noticed that the terrain had changed from steep mountainside to a gentle slope. Charles saw a patch of light through the forest. He looked up and as he got closer he saw it was a clearing where the stream crossed under the road. The light was the cleared road and ocean beyond. He was getting out of the forest! A feeling of joy overtook him. He surged forward to close the remaining few yards.

As he pulled the travail over the bank of the stream at the edge of the road, a car sped down the road toward them. Charles tried to shout at it to stop but there was no voice in his throat. The car kept going. Charles stopped at the side of the road totally dismayed. Suddenly the car's brake lights lit up and it screeched to a stop with all four wheels locked. With a grinding of gears then a whining noise the car drove backwards to Charles.

"Yes, indeed! I reckon you're the lost boys we heard about on the radio!" a tall lanky man said, jumping out of the passenger seat. "Come 'n help me, Jake," he yelled at the driver. "Don't be such a dumb ass. You almost didn't stop."

Charles and Robert were loaded into the back seat of the car and driven at top speed to the only doctor in the town, five miles away. Charles remembered the doctor sticking a long needle in his arm before he went to sleep.

He woke up in a hospital. There was nobody around when his eyes opened. A short time later a nurse in a starched white uniform and cap walked by and noticed him watching her. She came over to the side of his bed smiling. "Is Robert okay?" Charles asked.

She turned around, still smiling, without saying a word, and went back the way she came. A minute later she reappeared with a procession of doctors behind her. "Your friend will be all right, thanks to you," she said. "The doctors want to examine you now that you're awake." Charles was prodded and poked until every square inch of his body had been examined to see if it hurt or not. Finally they left and the visitors were allowed to come in.

His father was first. Charles had never seen him cry before. He had always thought that grown men could not cry, yet here was big Tom with tears in his eyes telling him how glad he was that his Little Charlie was okay after what he had been through. Ralph was also there thanking Charles for saving Robert's life. He kept repeating over and over that Charles had done a very smart thing for a city boy.

Chapter Fifteen

Tom's Secret

The hospital stay was short and eventful. Charles was not allowed to leave his bed for the first two days. Rose and June called every day to get the details of his escape and to make sure he was doing well. Charles did not tell them how dangerous the trip out of the mountains was, but Tom filled them in on the ordeal. The bandages on his head were changed routinely and his condition improved. He began to recognize his regular doctor and nurses. Charles wanted to visit Robert but for the first two days the nurses informed him that the boy was in very serious condition and it was best to leave him alone. His visitors reminded Charles that Robert had come close to death.

The most important part of his hospital stay was the opportunity to talk with his father during the long visits. One thing had bothered Charles since he had arrived at the farm, and he was determined to use this opportunity to resolve it. On the second day in the hospital Charles tried to get his answer.

"Father," he said, when they had run out of things to say, "Why did you leave the farm? The farm and people are so nice I don't see why anybody would want to go to the city or anyplace else to make a living."

"I was wonderin' when you'd ask about that. I reckon you like it here at the farm. Well, I knowed that after yes'day I'd sooner or later tell you the story." Tom was being very careful with his words. He was recalling events that changed his world many years ago. It was hard for him to begin. Once he started talking he felt he would never be able to stop.

"When I lived at the farm it weren't much different from what you see now. Oh, the house was newer 'n there were dozens of lobster traps 'n a barn to build. The fishery would give us new herrin' nets without charge so long as we'd sell them the catch. We'd use the nets mostly to catch bait for lobsters but now and then we'd get a big catch of herrin' 'n they'd buy them along with the lobsters. We're able to get by. The whole family was very happy. We're jest able to make a living and still claim our independence." Tom paused as he got closer to the answer that he had hidden from himself in the bad years.

He continued, "When I was about your age I found I was pretty handy with mechanical things. There was very little that I wouldn't take apart 'n fix easy as can be, whether it needed it or not. It was a real God-given gift to be able to use my hands so well. My mother used to say my fixin' things was as easy as falling off a log. As I got older, people would bring things to the house for me to fix. I got big-headded. I began to think I was almighty better than the other people at this here place. I got very restless and carried away with my ability to make things work." Tears swelled in the corners of his eyes as he stopped talking for a moment. He coughed and continued.

"One day I had a fearful fight with my father. I'd made some money repairing the major blade bearings in the town sawmill. The owner had ordered the bearings from the manufacturer... nobody knew how to install them. They'd sent for me 'n I was able to figure out how to remove the worn-out bearings 'n put the new ones in proper. I was only eighteen years old 'n the family couldn't get used to the idea of me being able to earn money on my own. I were really proud of myself because I read the diagrams that came with the sawmill equipment 'n borried the tools I needed from the garage 'n blacksmith shop in town. At any rate, my father told me that if I didn't need the family I could pack my almighty bags 'n live on my own."

Charles didn't interrupt his father. He was so fascinated by Tom's story of how he evolved from childhood to manhood that he could only purse his lips and listen.

His father continued, "I'd heard about the new farm machinery being introduced in the wheat fields in Manitoba and Saskatchewan 'n decided to head out there 'n make a life of my own instead of settling down on the farm like everybody else. There weren't any way a team of horses could hold me back after the fight with my father. I left and moved cross country doing odd jobs everywhere along the way 'n learning whatever I could about being a mechanic. Being a mechanic is a very honorable profession. The Wright brothers were mechanics 'n not only made their own airplane, but bilt the engine that ran it as well. I determined to be the best mechanic in the world 'n worked hard to learn the trade.

"Finally, I arrived in the plains provinces 'n found my dreams come true. Everybody were buying the new mechanical tractors, trucks, 'n reaping equipment 'n nobody knowed how to keep 'em running. This here new generation of gasoline-driven equipment were replacing the poor steam equipment from the turn of the century. Much of the old equipment were horse-driven 'n took up to sixty horses or mules to pull some of the combines. 'Specially since it takes an acre to feed a horse, everybody was replacing them as fast as new equipment were available to free more land for production. It were a revolution in farming." Tom smiled as he remembered the days of travel, change and the great energy that drove him on in his youth.

"Within five years I'd established a fine business where people would bring their equipment to me for repairs or I'd send my people out to the fields to repair it. Those be the good years. Then I got ambitious and bought a dealership to sell the equipment I was fixin' 'n did even better.

"One day I met your mother. She were very beautiful. The daughter of the largest farmer in the province. Her family were educated 'n spoke fancy English. I met her as I were repairing a tractor that I'd sold her father. I were much older than your mother. I'd never felt a need to get married or attached to one woman before. I had lots of money then. Every girl in town were after me. I remember romancing your mother that summer I met her. I bought a new Buick touring car to impress her 'n we'd go riding all over the country together. Finally, she give in 'n married me. Those be the good times." Tom's face saddened with thought.

He meditated for a minute before he continued, remembering. 'He was riding in the yellow touring car with the top down. His hard-yellow straw hat was firmly on his head (the felt hats did not stay on in the wind); there was always a girl by his side. The girls would wear thin light dresses with ribbons streaming from their hats and long hair as they drove through the dirt roads of the countryside. There were picnics by the side of the road, singing and laughter. He was tanned and muscular. The fresh country air was invigorating and made every cell in his body come alive. In the fall, after the harvest was in, there were weeks of celebration in the fields and at the various farms where he'd worked. The farmers weren't city fools. They didn't work all the time. There were seasons to plant and seasons to harvest. Everybody worked very long hours every day except Sunday during those seasons. There were also seasons to sit back and enjoy the fruits of their labor. These were the rewards for the toils of the long days and evenings when the sun would not set until late night over Northern skies.'

"Then the Depression came. One day I were making lots of money 'n had a span-new car 'n not a problem in the world. The next day not a body were paying their bills 'n the whole sky fell down. The Depression were a time of eternal darkness giving off no rays of hope. Your mother's family lost their farm to the bankers when they fell behind on the mortgage 'n equipment payments. After holding on for a few years, I lost the business. A beat man, I moved to the city to find work 'n you know the rest."

Tom was finished. He sighed. After all these years he had finally disclosed what was inside him to his son. He had never told his son of his successes. All Charles had seen was his failure to provide a better living for his family.

"Charles, I'm not blamin' myself for when I left this here place, 'cause a man must do what he feels inside him. I miss the freedom 'n good times I had before the Depression destroyed everything around me. I hope you'll have a fair chance to do whatever you want when you get older. I know'd after the trip down the mountain you're as capable as me and perhaps more. An act of courage like yours or my leaving the farm isn't done because a body tells you to do it. It comes from within."

Charles was at a loss for words to say to the proud man. He was surprised his father had traveled all over the place and even had his own business. Charles had no idea that his father had left the farm to be successful. He now felt that anything was possible and even he could travel when he grew up. Finally, he blurted out:

"Dad, I'm glad you told me. Maybe I shouldn't worry so much about the future. I'm proud to be your son."

They embraced before Tom left and Charles found himself wiping tears away afterward.

At last they let him up to visit Robert. Poor Robert had his leg in a cast and his head in bandages like Charles.

"Gosh, we look like wounded soldiers from a war movie," Charles commented when he saw Robert. Charles was in a good mood because he was going home soon and he did not want seeing Robert to spoil it.

"I hear you lugged me down the mountain 'n saved my life. Thanks for helping me." Robert struggled for the right words. He had never been so helpless in his life. Now he had to even thank little Charles for saving him. "How did you figger out a way to carry me out." he asked.

"I remembered an Indian movie where they used to move things on sticks. It seemed the only thing I could do to get you out of there. Gosh, I'm sorry that the Winchester got busted. It was a nice rifle. I'm glad you're okay. I thought you were going to die on me before I could get help."

Robert smiled. He still hurt from head to toe, but he was happy that it was Charles he had gone up the mountain with. He held out his hand.

"Let's be friends forever. Like blood brothers." Robert was very serious. He and Charles had a life bond together.

Charles grasped his hand and sealed the friendship.

The next week Charles was back in school. Everybody was asking him why his head was bandaged up. He told them he had an accident in Canada on a hunting trip. He didn't give them the details. They didn't need to know.

He had been going to school almost a week before he had the courage to tell Mary Anne the whole story. He even told her how he used the metric clock to get the extra strength and time to survive. She could hardly believe the tale. When she got home she told her mother, but her mother did not believe it either. She had not known Charles to tell tales, so one evening shortly afterward Mary Anne's mother visited Rose and got the whole story. Soon it had traveled throughout the neighborhood. The gang learned what had happened and afterward they followed Charles around asking for the details over and over. It took several weeks and the removal of the head bandage for the excitement to die down. Charles wanted only to be left in peace. But an ugly scar on his forehead remained as a souvenir of his fateful hunting trip.

***

One evening there was a terrible thunderstorm. The windows rattled and rain poured in torrents. Lightning lit up the sky nearby with violent thunderclaps following. Suddenly, there was a bright flash of lightning with a concurrent crash of thunder. The lights went out. Tom went outside to see if there was damage to the house. A few minutes later he was back inside and quite excited.

"Come here, lightning hit the tree in front of Harry's house. The big elm tree at Harry's house is split clean in half!"

Charles put on his yellow raincoat and was outside in a minute. Sure enough, the tree was split down the middle with half of it stretched out over the street. Charles did not go near because some wires had come down with it. Harry came out and together they stared at the giant tree that split in two as if an axe had struck it.

"Wow, that sure was a close call," Harry said, when he saw how the tree had almost struck the house. "I'm sure glad the tree fell in the street instead of the house!"

They stood together in front of Mary Anne's house discussing the magnitude of the awesome event as the rain continued to pour over them. Suddenly there was a great flash which knocked them over by a giant hand of force accompanied by a great crashing noise. They lay on the ground a minute before getting up.

"Are you okay?" Harry asked Charles as he helped him up.

"I'm okay." Charles answered. "Gee, what happened? Did we get struck by lightning?"

Harry was looking at the place where the great tree used to be.

"We didn't get struck but the tree did. The lightning knocked the rest of the tree over. The other half of the tree is on my house now!"

They ran over as Harry's mother and father rushed out of the house to inspect the damage. They were looking out the front window at the first strike and now were aghast at the damage caused a few minutes later. The tree had crushed the side and roof of the house as it fell down. There was nothing anyone could do. Harry was called back by his parents to find buckets for the water leaking inside. Charles went home.

There was much talk about the storm the next day at school. The twice-struck tree provided a new source of excitement and main topic of conversation, eclipsing even Charles' brush with death.

Chapter Sixteen

The Apple War

The morning air was brisk. On the way to school the children would walk fast to stay warm looking forward to the warm schoolhouse. After school the long summer nights were gone making it easier to stay home evenings as the atmosphere cooled. The day after the thunderstorm was no exception because the morning rain was cold. It had stopped raining by the time school got out.

After school the children played around the downed tree. This was an unusual opportunity to climb through branches while on the ground, and to assess the size of the giant at that level. The tow truck arrived and men with chainsaws proceeded to make firewood of the elm. Harry's father stayed home to make arrangements for house repairs. Between phone calls he sawed away at his tree-half with a bucksaw and stacked the wood in the backyard. Harry had the task of moving wood into the cellar afterward. In the meantime, his father kept him busy trimming small branches from logs with a clumsy handsaw.

Charles hung around the tree side activity for a while until realizing that he was in the way of the workers. He retired to his backyard, which was covered with apples knocked down by the storm. All during the year apples had fallen prematurely because of worm infestation. The honey wagon horses did not seem to mind the worms, for they ate all the green apples they could find at ground level or within reach of their yellow front molars. Now the remainder were lying on the ground. Charles picked up a few and threw them at the other tree. They were ripe but none were edible. He knew his mother would expect him to clean the yard up.

Charles went into the cellar and dragged out his red wagon. He proceeded to fill it with downed apples. When he had the wagon full he left it in place and came in for dinner.

That evening he visited Adam.

"Hey, Adam, you know that apple tree that you have in the backyard?" Charles asked.

"So, what about it?" Adam responded, wondering why Charles had come by this late in the day.

"Let's take a look at it." Charles said as he led Adam around the side of the house. They went around the back and in the light from the kitchen window it was evident the yard was strewn with apples. "Are your parents going to make you pick them up?"

"I was hoping that they wouldn't notice them." Adam said trying to ignore the obvious.

"I have a great idea." Charles said, knowing that the idea was precise, logical, and a lot of fun. "Everybody has a yard full of apples that have to picked up sooner or later. The later they get collected the more rotten the apples will be." Charles was envisioning what they would look like if they were all allowed to get rotten before they were collected. "I think we should have an apple war!" Charles declared.

"Do you mean a real war with the rest of the gang?" Adam's eyes lit up at the idea of throwing messy apples around.

"Naw. I mean a war with the Baker Street gang. We can fill our wagons with apples and meet them someplace!"

"That's a great idea. We can meet them on their street so our parents won't get mad at us and make us clean up the mess afterward. Let's have a meeting tomorrow and come up with a plan." Adam was elated. He had been looking forward to getting into trouble for months since the marsh expedition and had not had a decent opportunity until now.

Charles went home with a smile. He decided he was going to have a good time while he was still a boy, because someday he would be grown up and have to work all the time. He knew that parents never have any fun.

The next day the gang gathered at the clubhouse. Everybody was there including Richard, who was back from his summer leave. Adam was the first to broach the new proposal.

"Kids, Charles had an idea that we can have an apple war with the Baker Street gang. He said our parents won't mind if we do it away from here." His enthusiasm was evident. He had also talked to Merle to make sure that he had some support.

Harry intervened, "What are you talking about? Let Charles tell us what he has in mind." Harry showed no enthusiasm. He would not commit himself until he had heard the whole plan.

Charles now had everybody's attention. "I think it's a swell idea to load up our wagons with apples and have a real war with the Baker Street gang. We have to pick up the apples anyway 'cause the storm knocked them all down. Most of them are old and ripe and won't hurt anybody. If we have the war on their street we'll be getting rid of the apples at the same time. It'll be just like a snowball fight only with apples." Charles had infected the gang with his enthusiasm. It would be hard to resist the temptation to raise hell in such a relatively harmless way.

"I say no." It was Harry speaking. He had a habit of getting in the way of a good time. "I don't have an apple tree and therefore don't have an apple problem. My parents are unhappy over the tree damage and I don't want to upset them with anything else."

"My backyard is covered with rotten apples," Richard was giving his professional opinion. "I can't think of a better way to get rid of them than in an apple war."

"Let's take a vote on it," Charles suggested, knowing that everybody had an apple tree except Harry. That was why the night before, he had gone to Adam instead.

The vote was four to one. Harry decided not to join the battle. Since he had no apple tree he was excused from the operation. He listened in as the four boys started planning the conflict. A few minutes later the boys left to visit Jack, the Baker Street Gang leader.

Jack was home when the four boys gathered outside his front door.

"Hey, What do you kids want?" he asked suspiciously. It was rare to find such a representation from the Marsh Street gang at his doorstep.

Adam motioned for him to come outside so his parents wouldn't overhear the conversation. They met on the lawn.

Charles was short and to the point.

"Don't you have an apple tree in your backyard?" Charles knew he did because he had looked over the fence from Mary Anne's yard once to see what was there.

"Sure, I do. So, what?" Jack was being defensive because he had no idea what the plan was.

"Well, we had a meeting and decided that since everybody had apple trees, there was a heck of a mess to pick up after the storm." Charles paused for Jack to digest the information. "We decided that we could collect all the apples from our street and have an apple war with your gang. It would be just like a snowball fight only with apples instead."

Jack stared at them for a few seconds and then lit up. His face grew a big grin.

"Great, I'll have to meet with the gang. I'll get back with you tomorrow. It seems like a good idea if I can get the other kids to go along with it."

"Meet us at Harry's clubhouse at five o'clock tomorrow," Adam concluded.

The next day the Marsh Street gang, without Harry who was still loading firewood into his cellar, was filling their wagons and bushel baskets, supplied by Charles. Some of the apples were quite rotten and the boys were careful to handle them last and place them closest to the top of the wagons and baskets. A plan evolved. They could get more apples in two baskets in a wagon than they could get in the wagon if they piled them in loose. However, there was a shortage of bushel baskets. It was decided to fill the wagons and then come back for the bushel baskets after the war started. There were not enough apples to fill all the baskets and wagons so one wagon was left empty to transport the baskets to a closer point to the battle zone when they knew where it was to be.

At precisely five o'clock, Jack and one of his gang showed up at the clubhouse. Harry was also there, not wanting to miss the meeting even if he was not to be a part of the scheme.

Jack opened the discussion:

"I met with my gang and we decided to have the war. The gang and I decided that it has to be on your street. We don't want to get stuck cleaning up the mess afterward." He was giving them his terms. If they wanted the war it had to be on Marsh Street territory.

Charles looked at Merle. That was not the plan. The plan was to get rid of the apples, not to acquire twice as many of them in the process.

Merle had a solution.

"There's a stretch on Baker Street where there aren't any houses. You know, down the street below the hill where the street ends. Why not meet there where nobody will notice us?"

Jack thought for a minute. 'If they held the war in front of somebody's house, the conflict could be stopped short by any one of the neighbors that saw them. The deserted end of the street could work.' He looked at his associate. The other boy nodded approval and took Jack outside for a private discussion. Jack returned with a smile. The war was approved:

"Okay, the war is on. Let's make it an hour after school is out the day after tomorrow. We get the end of the street." They shook hands.

The next day the children feverishly prepared for the war. They transported the bushel baskets to Ralph's house, which was closest to the war zone, and hid them under some bushes on the lawn so his mother would not get suspicious. Then they went to Merle's house and found cardboard boxes to fabricate into shields. The shields were reinforced with thin lath sticks for support and to provide a handhold in the middle. Richard had been lucky and located a bushel basket cover of strong, but thin, plywood. There was hardly enough time to paint or draw anything on them with crayons. The boys had many ideas and suggestions from a recent Crusades movie that they had seen. Adam painted a cross on his shield but did not have enough time to embellish it properly. Charles drew a bulls-eye on his, and with crayons Richard drew a lion ended up looking like a dog. Merle drew crossed Indian tomahawks and nailed some of his sister's ribbons to the handles. Finally, the moment came to move and they converged at the end of Baker Street.

What they saw dismayed them. They found out why the other gang had decided on the end of the street for their position. They had barricaded it with boxes, boards, and plywood. Charles looked at the obstacle with dismay.

"Gosh, What did we get ourselves into?" he asked Richard, who was pulling a wagon next to him. Richard gave him a sad look and they advanced into the battle with an Indianwarcry.

The apples started arriving from the barricade long before they were within range. The Baker Street gang was anxious and had stockpiled quite a bit of ammunition. As the Marsh Street gang got closer, the battle started in earnest. Apples began flying in all directions. Some of them were soft and rotten, others hard as rocks. They bounced off barricades, heads, shields, feet, knees, and began to cover the street with pulp. The battle wore on as the wagons emptied. The Marsh Street gang kept at a maximum distance from the barricades to lessen the impact of the incoming missiles. Charles, because he could not throw as far as the other kids since he was smallest, was sent for more ammunition. He raced to Richard's house with the empty red wagon trailing behind him. Once there, he wrestled the baskets on the wagon and picked up the spillage. He tore back to the war zone.

The battle went on stronger than ever. The Marsh Street gang was getting the worst of it because they were exposed in the middle of the street with only their shields to hide behind. Merle slipped on a rotten apple and went down. A cheer went up from the Baker Street gang and they concentrated their firepower on the distraught boy. Merle crawled out of range to scrape the apple pulp off his clothes and neck. Another wagon emptied sending Charles to the back lines again. When he returned it was time for another trip. The Marsh Street gang had spent a great effort picking up apples. There had been eight-bushel baskets of apples stored under the bush in addition to the three wagon-loads. Now Charles was making the fourth and last trip.

The street was covered with apples, fragments, and pulp. The children were getting tired of throwing them. Their arms ached and muscles were sore. So far nobody was hurt but some of the children had some sore spots where they had been hit in unprotected places. The shields and barricades were covered with the splash from rotten apples. They dripped with pulp and juice. The cardboard shields were torn and the lath sticks holding them together had broken. The Marsh Street gang threw the shields away and hid behind the up-ended wagons as they took the bushel baskets of apples from Charles when he arrived.

The bushel baskets were running low when the Baker Street gang ran out of ammunition. They were trapped. Worse than that, they had to leave the barricade to pick up the apples lying in the street in front of them. The Marsh Street gang had a clear advantage now because they could pick up apples from around them when the basket supply ran out. The tide of battle changed as the Baker Street gang got plastered for the first time. The only thing that saved them from total destruction was the tired arms of the Marsh Street children and, ultimately, oncoming darkness.

When the battle broke off, the children headed home with their empty wagons rattling behind them. They were very tired and happy. Nobody had been hurt. The battlefield was thick with smashed apples and the rotten pulp. Charles collected his baskets and snuck them into his cellar with his wagon before his father could see them. He ran directly into the bedroom to change his clothes and washed the pulp off his arms and hair in the bathroom before his mother could question what happened to him, though she was suspicious when she saw his wet hair and mischievous grin.

The next evening June made a comment at the dinner table about a big mess on Baker Street that somebody had seen. The whole end of the street was reported to be covered with rotten apples. She looked at Charles, knowing he probably had something to do with it. Charles gave her his usual innocent grin.

Chapter Seventeen

Sweet Revenge

*A*s Charles walked to school with Mary Anne the next morning, fallen leaves swirled around their feet. The maple and elm trees were rapidly becoming skeletons. Charles picked up a handful of maple leaves. He studied the red and yellow colors on them and peeled away the thin brittle leaf between the veins.

"Look how beautiful they are, Mary Anne. The colors are changing. Soon they will be gone and buried in the snow. I wonder what life would be like without the four seasons. I think the change is as important as the beauty that comes with it. I even look forward to winter because it's different from summer and when I get tired of winter there's spring to look forward to. Do you like the fall as much as I do?"

Mary Anne kicked a windblown pile of leaves that lay in her path.

"Heck, no, I don't like it. It means that things are dying. I hate winter and this cold weather means that it's not far away. I especially hate the cold mornings." She blew a small cloud of frosty air from her lungs and watched it evaporate in front of her. Soon she would be wearing gloves and earmuffs to and from school. She thought about the purple grapes hanging from the grape arbor at Charles' house. The sour grapes had not been picked and were now wrinkled and shriveled up. That was a sign of winter to Mary Anne. Winter was when things got old and wrinkled and ugly.

"I love the spring. I love to see things start to grow all over again and feel the ground warm up. I love flowers and pretty things. I also love you and am glad that you didn't die when you were in Canada.

Boys and men are always in trouble or getting killed. I hope that you won't die on me before we grow up."

She heard about Merle falling into the saltwater channel in the marsh. His sister found out from him and told the other girls in one of their gossip sessions. Of the gang, only Harry never got in trouble. He never took chances and would probably live to be a hundred years old. She sometimes felt the boys were trying to get themselves killed before they had a chance to grow old as people were supposed to. She was glad that her place was in the home. It was safer there.

The new classroom teacher was much older than Miss Pritchett. Mrs. Boothby was married. She was worn out and lacked the enthusiasm of the younger teachers. She never looked forward to the classroom full of strange faces each September. Each year she would have to learn all of their names and hold them captive in her room whether or not they cared to learn anything. Patience was not one of her virtues. She was an inflexible and rigid disciplinarian who believed that her job was to teach by rote and not expect anything in return from her students unless it was exactly what she gave out.

The new lot of students was just like the class she had endured for the past year. Only their names were different. After several weeks of class, she was getting used to matching the names with the seating plan she kept inside her attendance and grading book. One child had a scar on his forehead. 'He appeared quiet in class but could be a troublemaker,' she thought. 'Maybe he had been in a fight and got all scarred up. What a way to start out in life. I should find out what his problem is so I can keep him away from the other children and from disrupting the class,' she decided.

One afternoon as the class was filing out of the door to go home, she stopped him.

"Charles," she said skeptically, "tell me how you got that scar on your face."

Charles looked back at Mary Anne who was unable to wait for him because of the grouping arrangement that took the children to their street.

"Mrs. Boothby, I got it in a hunting accident when I was in Canada," Charles said nervously, trying to get to the door and catch up with the other children.

The teacher looked at him fiercely in the eye.

139

"You're lying! You're too young to go hunting. Why do you make up stories like that? Can't you think of anything better to tell me? Did you get in a fight with the other boys?"

Charles didn't know what to say. He knew by her tone of voice that she would never believe him no matter what he said.

"I'm telling you the truth. You can ask my mother if you want." Charles had said all he wanted. He did not want to argue with the old flint.

"You go and stand in the corner for lying to me. There's no need to call your mother because she would cover up for you. I want you to stand in the corner every day until you tell me the truth." She pointed to the corner of the room farthest from the windows.

Charles had no choice but to obey. He stood in the corner alone with his thoughts while the teacher went out of the room. He thought of the children going home without him. After an endless period of time the teacher returned. She ignored him for several minutes as she got her things together. Finally, she told him to go home.

"When you have the truth for me, I'll let you go home with the rest of the children," she said sternly. She would show him who was in charge of things in this room.

Charles ran halfway home before he caught up with the troop. Mary Anne didn't believe him when he told her why he'd been left behind. Charles hardly believed it himself. He didn't want to tell his mother because he knew he would have to solve the problem, though in his own time. Charles realized the solution would not lie in events at the school and that he would have to find his own answers, in his special time, for the misled autocrat.

Every night for a week the teacher would interrogate Charles and then exile him to the corner for punishment. She started looking for small excuses to stay later before she would let him go. She would now erase the blackboards after school instead of when she came in the mornings. There was always paperwork that could be graded or completed before she went home instead of taking it with her. Charles stayed later and later until he could no longer catch up with the group of children being herded home. Sometimes she would have him carry things to her car where she would put her grading book in the glove compartment and other things on the front seat.

He began to hate the class and especially Mrs. Boothby. It was time for him to plan some revenge. When he was standing in the corner he would shut his eyes and think to himself. Mrs. Boothby, you're in the sixty minutes of school time and I'm going to reach outside to my Metric Clock time and find your master. Day after day he suffered his corner ordeal until one day his sister gave him the answer he needed.

One evening Charles was looking at some papers his sister had brought home from school. She started talking about her biology class. They were dissecting frogs in a laboratory room. Charles was fascinated by the treatment of the creatures. June noticed his interest and announced that she had a science project for the class that would entail studying the feeding habits of mice and what they would do to get fed. "Do you mean live mice?" Charles asked.

"Sure," June answered in response to Charles' eagerness to learn about her work at school. "I'm going to buy one in the pet department of the five-and-dime store downtown."

The next day in class Mrs. Boothby was discussing her favorite subject—amoeba.

"They're everywhere," she stated, noticing that the class's attention was glued to the rough drawing she made of one on the blackboard. "Particularly in water that has not been boiled to kill them. They're deadly and will kill people with all kinds of diseases if they are allowed to live. They are the germs that live in water and are as deadly as the germs carried by mosquitoes and the fleas on rats and mice." She grimaced at the thought of fleas jumping on her from rats or mice.

The class noticed her reaction to the subject matter. Charles paid special attention to her sensitivity. Then she went on about the disease carrier fleas carried by the rats of the Bubonic Plague during the Dark Ages. When she finished, the whole class was silent with awe at the terrible things that grew, swam, or hopped around them. Charles was very impressed.

At the end of class she kept Charles behind as usual. She let him stay at his seat now instead of standing him in the corner. She enjoyed seeing him squirm in his seat as he watched the other children leave without him. She left the room. Charles closed his eyes and invoked his Metric Clock, searching for a solution to the problem. The answer came. Charles started to draw pictures of rats

141

on a piece of plain paper. When she returned a half-hour later the paper was covered with rats. She got a glimpse of his work as she let him leave the room.

"What have you drawn on the paper?" she asked.

"Just some amoeba," Charles answered as he looked her in the eye.

Charles didn't go directly home that afternoon. He stood at the bus stop for a while until he got a ride to the town square. Woolworth's five-and-dime store had just what he wanted. They had white mice and brown guinea pigs.

"I want them," he told the clerk. "All of them." The young lady gave him a strange look as she opened the top of the case.

"Are you sure you want all of them?" she asked. "There are at least a dozen rats here. I also have about ten mice. What are you going to do with them?"

"My sister and brother are in college and they need to do experiments with them for their biology classes," Charles coolly answered. He took three dollars from his pipe tobacco box and paid the girl.

She packaged them in separate cardboard boxes. She could not help notice the odd smile on his face as he left. 'He's really strange,' she thought as she shuddered from handling the rodents.

That evening Charles replaced the boxes with two more durable wooden White Owl cigar boxes and hid them under the front porch after placing an old rag in each box to keep the rodents warm and alive. He didn't bother to feed or water them. 'It won't matter,' he thought. 'They'll be wilder if they're hungry and thirsty.' He took out the largest mouse and put it in a cup with a saucer over it in his sister's room and a note on it to preclude accidents. She would be pleased that he got the rodent for her.

Charles had trouble sleeping that night. He imagined his special clock. In his special time all he could think of was the white rats and mice. He envisioned Mrs. Boothby in a little box and thousands of flea-covered rodents crawling all over her. He fell asleep with a wicked smile on his face.

The next morning Charles rushed out of the house, gathered up his boxes and ran all of the way to school. He was the first student there. He hid behind a tree on the edge of the small parking lot at the side of the school. The only car in the lot belonged to the janitor who always arrived early to fill the furnace and heat the building up. Shortly afterward Mrs. Boothby arrived in her 1935 two-door Ford coupe. The car had a very small front seat with an oval rear window directly over the back. The back end of the car was a large rumble seat that opened outside where the back seat and trunk would be on most cars. She opened the glove compartment and took out her attendance and grade book. Then she went into the school.

As soon as she went around the corner Charles opened the door to her car and the glove compartment. It was half full of papers and maps. He emptied it throwing the contents under the front seat. He looked inside one box of rodents. They were all milling around and restless from not being fed or watered. Then he took the boxes of mice and rats stuffing them inside the glove compartment until it was so full that it was all he could do to cram the last one inside. He jumped out of the car and carefully dropped the boxes into a trash can behind the school. At least they'll keep each other warm, he grinned. Then he joined some children who had just arrived.

That day in class was the longest that Charles ever remembered. He seemed immersed in thought as Mrs. Boothby droned on about the various subjects. Charles even managed to smile while enduring the ordeal of the Reinhart alphabet letter drawing session. At the end of class, she could not help but notice his smile.

"What's bothering you today?" she asked sarcastically.

"My sister just sent in an application for the National Honor Society and I'm glad for her." Charles answered, looking her squarely in the eye.

"I don't know how you could have such a talented sister," she stated. Go home now. I have seen enough of you today."

Charles lingered around the front of the school before heading toward home. Mrs. Boothby threw her grade book on the front seat with her purse as she drove out of the school lot heading the other way. As she approached the intersection at the street light she reached over to open the glove compartment of the car. Traffic was heavy because Main street crossed the road that led across the marsh and carried much of the traffic from the city beyond into the country. As she slowed down for the red light the glove compartment opened and twenty-one terrified, hungry, thirsty, and unhappy rats and mice jumped out into the front seat and on her.

Charles was watching from the sidewalk. He had begun to believe she would never open the glovebox. He didn't hear her scream, but he did see her car drive right into the flow of traffic going the other way. A big black Packard almost ran into the side of the little car forcing it into the sidewalk. Mrs. Boothby threw the coupe door open to escape the torrent of rodents crawling over her. When the crowd gathered a few minutes later to see what happened all of her antagonists had scurried away.

For the remainder of the week the principal taught the class. He informed the class their teacher had been in a very serious accident and probably would not be back to teach before the week was out. He scowled and commented that he would be happy if she never returned to the classroom. He had never liked her but found the rat story too much to believe. The man was glad to see her leave. Charles was not the only person glad to see old prune face gone.

The next week Mrs. Boothby returned. She looked very tired and worn out. She had begun thinking of taking an early retirement to escape from the job she hated so much. Nobody believed her rat story and she could not imagine who could have done it. Certainly not one of the children in her class. She decided to let Charles go home with the rest of the children. She was anxious to get home and forget the classroom. The pleasure of tormenting Charles had vanished.

Several weeks later at a parent-teachers conference Mrs. Boothby met Rose. Rose inquired about Charles' schoolwork.

"Charles does good work but he needs to quit telling stories," she responded.

"He has always had a great imagination. I'll talk to him about telling tales. I'm very concerned about his health at this time. He has occasional headaches from that accident in Canada. I hope they don't interfere with his schoolwork or classroom behavior."

Mrs. Boothby's curiosity was aroused.

"Was the accident from a fight with another child?" she asked with a trace of a scowl.

"Oh, no," Rose answered. "He was hunting with his cousin in Canada and they fell off a cliff into a large stream. The other boy was unconscious for two days and Charles dragged him off the mountain by himself. He was a hero in those parts and there was even a big article written in the local paper at the time about how he saved the

144

other boy." She looked at the teacher with surprise. "Do you mean that nobody told you about him?" she asked.

Mrs. Boothby flushed and looked away from Rose.

"No," she lied, "nobody ever told me." Her mind raced over the treatment she had subjected Charles to. 'I hope nobody finds out that I've punished him for nothing,' she thought. 'It seems hard to believe that the kid is a hero of any kind. My main concern is that he or the other students do not inform this woman about my treatment. Although it's against my principles, I'll have to be nice to him to keep him from telling on me.'

After the meeting she began to take an interest in Charles. She noticed he was always ahead in the reading assignments, so she brought in books from her own collection for him to read. She began to feel guilty for punishing him and decided to make it up to him by giving him things from her home to read. He readily read David Copperfield. The Last of the Mohicans, and many other books that she assigned to him. He was able to read anything she gave him. 'He must have taught himself to read,' she thought. 'His mind is years ahead of his body.' She took a real liking to Charles and was the one person, besides his parents, who realized that Charles was growing up.

Chapter Eighteen

The Spy's Lair

The fall season changed the countryside into waves of drifting leaves and sparkling cold mornings. Most of the deciduous trees were bare, stripped of their summer beauty. The newspapers were predicting a very cold winter. Mittens appeared on children's hands and leather gloves became popular with adults again. The War was becoming an object of study for historians. Only occasional bits of news would appear in the papers or on the news clips. The War trials were in full motion and the only remaining War news was an infrequent story about War criminals being discovered and imprisoned. Israel was escaping from British domination and entering her first war for independence. Germany, Italy, and Japan were rapidly becoming allies while the old ally Russia was now the enemy. Russia readily assumed the Nazi role of the Satanic bad country. Times had not changed, the players had.

June was in her senior year of high school. She dropped the piano lessons to her mother's economic relief and esthetic grief. June now had only one boyfriend. It was not by her choice but by his dominance that the others were kept at bay. She had found her match.

Tom still wore his hard-yellow straw hat. He was not about to discard what he grew up with without good cause for the soft felt hats that first appeared thirty years before. His hat was a reminder of better times, of open touring cars and girls with lacy dresses. Now his job was improving. When he first went to work during the Depression, it was as a machinist's helper in the plant—the only work he could find. Now his older natural skills had come into play and his role had evolved to that of an equipment mechanic and finally to the head of the department. Although he was still powerful physically, he knew he was slowing down and appreciated the help of his assistants on some of the heavy shop work. He was able to use his mind more and his body less in his daily routine. His talents had evolved as he grew older and more experienced in his trade.

Rose had not changed. Her household routine was the same and would remain so until the day she envisioned arrived, when they would again own a family car. She started weekly driving lessons at a new driving school in town with the ultimate goal of being ready when the wheeled freedom was purchased. Rose longed for open spaces and travel that she remembered from her childhood. The small house was becoming confining to her. Vague memories of rides in the countryside in an open car with fresh spring breezes blowing through her hair would come back to her when she opened a window to air the stuffiness out of the house. She knew that sooner or later Tom would buy a car. Somehow, she could not convince him to buy one at this time. They were still scarce and expensive. 'There may be a reason other than economics that is holding him back from even looking at new cars,' she thought. 'Maybe he really likes riding to work on the bus, even though he complains about it.'

The neighborhood was also changing. A person living on Marsh Street would say things never change. An outsider would notice a few people moving in and out, a tree disappearing, houses being built in a few lots that were fields of weeds and grass before, and a new automobile in a driveway that previously had been empty. There was more traffic on Main Street... a long row of large concrete conduit lay side by side in a field to accommodate the increase in growth.

The gang had grown a little older and busy again with school. Harry now went to a different school in town and the rest of the gang saw very little of him. He also had a lot of homework to consume the time he used to spend with the other boys. The clubhouse was not used anymore. Harry had relinquished his leadership when he refused to participate in the apple war. The gang did not have a place to meet or Harry's conservative judgment for leadership. Otherwise, the gang was not leaderless because it still had Charles.

Charles was as quiet as ever. He never said anything unless he was sure of what he had to say. Because he had been shy before, many people did not notice a difference in him. But his shyness had been replaced by a quiet boldness.

There was one other change worth noting. Marking the change of season, to everyone's pleasure at the Wallace household, pumpkin and apple pies had replaced the rhubarb.

In mid-October, on the school grounds, a large boy from another part of town started pushing Charles around. Like Mrs. Boothby, he seemed to derive innate pleasure from bullying people. Poor Charles became a victim again, because of his small size. The pushing evolved to punching and kicking. As the violence grew, the pleasure of the large boy increased, proportionally. It did Charles no good to fight back because he was no physical match for the boy. After several weeks of increased bullying, Charles decided he needed to cure the problem. One afternoon he sat on the hard dirt bench under the elm tree. He invoked his metric clock and started daydreaming. The solution came in the image of a slingshot.

After school the next day he went into the cellar of his house and found a piece of thin metal pipe with wires inside. He pulled the wires out of the conduit and put it in the big vise on the workbench. Taking a hacksaw off a nail he proceeded to cut a foot-long section of the pipe off with the dull blade. After much trial and error beating and hammering on the pipe, he had created a metal slingshot. It was a simple vee shape with the pipe bent outward and upward about halfway up the length.

Next he took an old orange bicycle inner tube that had once seen duty on his sister's bike, and cut out a two-inch by twelve-inch section. He doubled the narrow section over and tied each end to the slingshot. It was firm but very elastic. Much more so than Merle's with the thick auto tire tube rubber. Charles found a round lead gutter pipe on a shelf. It had been used to connect the gutter to the drainpipe from the roof before Tom replaced it. From this he manufactured lead bullets about the thickness of his small finger. He made them about an inch long because they were easier to grip than round buckshot.

The next day the big kid hit Charles on the head above his scar. Charles' head began to hurt from the old injury. Tears came to his eyes.

He stammered, "Why don't you leave me alone? What's wrong with you?"

The big kid laughed at Charles' displeasure and promised him more for tomorrow. That afternoon Charles changed his clothes and went into the cellar to practice with his new weapon. He lined up some wooden boxes and penciled in rough bulls-eyes. The boxes were made of thin wood and had once contained produce. Charles piled them on top of the coal bin, which was low at this time, and went to the other end of the cellar. The light was very poor, but that did not bother him as he practiced away until dinner time. When he went upstairs he had forgotten his headache. At the end of the day, the lead shots were close to the bulls-eye and they all went through the wooden slats of the box. A few of the shots left small round holes, the rest of them made rectangular slots about an inch long from the shots turning end over end as they traveled to the target. The round-holed shots went through both sides of the box.

The next day the bully continued tormenting Charles. Charles did not seem to mind. This caused the boy to hit him harder. He looked the bully in the eye and said nothing. After school Charles did not go home with his group but followed the bully's group at a good distance. When they divided up, he got closer to the bully. The large kid smiled when he saw Charles, and strutted up to him.

"Didn't you get enough at the playground?" he yelled.

When he got close, Charles took the slingshot from under his shirt, pulled the rubber back as far as he could, and held it pointed at the bully's face. The big kid saw the lead projectile and turned pale. He put his hands over his face.

"Don't do it," he pleaded. He looked through his fingers and saw that Charles still had it pointed at him. There was absolutely no expression on Charles' face. Charles said nothing. The bully knew that he had met his match.

"O.K. I promise to leave you alone. I'm sorry I hurt you." He took his hands away from his face to show that he was sincere and not lying.

"You'd better mean it or I'll get you with this!" Charles coolly said as he turned the slingshot away. He let the projectile fly just past the bully's head, the half ounce of lead impaling itself in a high fence plank with a loud thunk. Then he turned around and went home. He knew the bully would not bother him again because force had been met with force and determination. The bully also knew that he could catch a lead projectile at night or from behind a tree when he least expected it.

The next day at school Charles anxiously waited for the boy at break time to see what would happen next. The boy did not appear. A day later the bully walked over to Charles. After looking eye to eye for a moment he put his hand out. Charles reluctantly shook hands. Charles learned the bully's name was George and George thought Charles had made the greatest slingshot on earth. Later on George found out how Charles got his scar and followed him around the schoolyard asking questions about his incredible adventure and how to make slingshots. Eventually, George's offer of friendship was accepted. He was someone to talk to besides the gang when Charles was at school. And he had passed the word around that Charles was fearless.

Soon it was Halloween. The neighborhood children were excited and looking forward to the night out. The classroom was decorated with the children's drawings of skeletons and pumpkins. Mrs Boothby, after having reassessed her personal affairs and attitudes toward teaching, had bought brilliantly colored decorations from the five-and-dime to decorate the remaining wall spaces in the room. After school, herds of children would roam the streets in search of candies on their demand.

Charles and Mary Anne had spent the day before carving faces out of perfectly good pumpkins to place on their front porches that evening with candles flickering through the jagged facial openings.

Charles met Mary Anne later that afternoon. They were anxious to start trick-or-treating. Charles wore old clothes, now torn, and with a makeshift hat and a broom, to carry, he became a scarecrow. Mary Anne wore a paper witch costume. They carried shopping bags to fill with candies and other loot. June was left behind in a grouchy mood to hand out candy, being too old to roam the streets. The pumpkins were lit again and the children turned loose on the neighborhood.

Charles and Mary Anne joined the torrent of screaming and joyous children. They went door to door making their threats and filling the shopping bags with rewards until they started reaching houses which were running out of treats to giveaway. The shopping bags were half full. It would take them some time to consume the supply of candy. Of course, the rest of the family would be happy to help.

They were getting tired and the evening cold air was being felt. The crowd of children had thinned out considerably by now. Mary Anne asked Charles if they could turn around and go home. They had reached an old part of town with very large houses on the Main Street. Charles agreed to turn around and they could work the other side of the street on the way home.

They stopped at a big old house on a rise. The house had a round widow's walk at the center of the roof where a person could look out over the whole area. The children knocked loudly on the door. A middle-aged woman came to the door. She looked out and smiled.

"Children, I'm out of candy," she said, "Let me get you some apples instead."

She went into the reaches of the house to get the apples from the kitchen. As they waited, Charles peered past the open door to see what the big house looked like. In the living room to the right a set of double doors was open. Charles stuck his head around the door and saw a man inside a large room with bookshelves covering one wall. There was a fireplace in the middle of another side. As he watched, the man turned around and Charles recognized the beak-like nose of the thin man he knew as the spy. The man smiled and walked through a door into the back of the house. A minute later the woman came through with the apples. Charles had backed up to the outside of the porch when Mary Anne took both of the apples. She turned around and noticed the strange look on Charles' face.

"What's wrong with you?" she asked.

"Gosh! The spy lives there! I saw him in the other room!" Charles' heart was pounding with excitement. "Don't eat the apples! They might be poisoned!" he warned.

"Are you sure?" Mary Anne asked calmly, not knowing whether to believe Charles or not.

"Gee, Wait until I tell the gang!" Charles exclaimed. He looked back at the house to note its location for the future.

They went directly home. Mary Anne was glad the day was over. She was tired and worn out from all the excitement. Charles had made her throw the apples away after they got out of sight of the big house. 'If that was not really the spy,' she thought, 'it was a waste of two perfectly good apples.'

After school the next day Charles met with the gang at his house. They unanimously agreed to visit the spy on Saturday morning. At the meeting Adam brought up a very good point.

"If the spy lives where you saw him," he asked Charles, "then why did we see him at a bus stop on the other side of town where we live?"

"Maybe that was to throw people off his trail by leading them away from his house," Charles answered, adding to the excitement.

That Saturday they banded together and headed out to the house on the rise on Main Street. Adam no longer carried a switch. The beehive had cured him of attacking things with it. The morning was cool and none of the children wore mittens or gloves. They slowed down when they saw the old house with the watchtower.

"Well, see the kind of house he has! Only a spy would live in a house like that!" Charles exclaimed.

The boys stopped talking and started whispering among themselves. They banded closer together. The house was on a corner lot. The children reached the corner and surveyed the house.

"What do we do now?" Richard asked as he stood in the knot of boys looking at the house and each other.

They were in a quandary. After reaching their objective they did not know what to do.

"I'll go over and ask for a glass of water to see if the spy is home," Merle volunteered.

The boys huddled on the corner as Merle knocked on the door. When the lady opened the door, Merle told her that he had been on a hike and was very thirsty. The kind lady motioned for him to come in. She saw the three other boys waiting outside.

"Go get your friends. I'll bet they're also thirsty," she said to Merle. Merle turned around and called them.

They reluctantly filed into the big house. The lady led them into a large kitchen. She bade them to sit down and went into a pantry to fill some glasses. She made two trips and gave them each a large glass full of water. Then she rustled around in the pantry again and came out with a plate heaped high with sugar cookies. The children had no fear of the woman. She was no different from anyone's mother. They looked around for the spy as they ate the cookies.

"I had a small boy about your age," the generous woman was saying. "He died of influenza many years ago." She was lonely and enjoyed having the children's company even if they did appear to be very nervous.

"What kind of work does your husband do?" Charles boldly asked. He knew he could trust her if the spy was not present.

"He works for the government," she said. "He travels a lot but he should be home shortly. He's an investigator for the new Federal Civil Aviation Bureau office in the city. His job is to investigate airplane problems and accidents." She saw that they were nervously looking into the other rooms of the house. "Where did you boys say you were from?" she asked to keep the conversation going.

"Marsh Street," Richard answered.

"Well, my husband and I lived near you for many years until we inherited this house from my mother this summer. Marsh Street is a nice place. We liked the area very much."

An automobile noise suddenly appeared close as a car drove over gravel into the driveway. Charles looked out the window and saw a brown Chevrolet come into view underneath. There was a U.S. Government license plate on the front. The man with the beak stepped out carrying an old leather briefcase. He did not appear so threatening as before.

"We need to go now," Merle stated as he heard the car drive in. The boys hastily got up and headed toward the front door. The lady followed them as the tall man came in behind her from the back. He took off his coat and rounded hat as he walked into the hallway where the boys were. The clothes and briefcase were placed on a chair. Adam could not help but notice that U.S. Government was stamped on the worn briefcase flap above the lock.

The man came up to them and smiled. Then he shook each of their hands before he let them go.

"I'm glad to meet such fine young men," he told them as they filed out. "Study hard at school so you can accomplish things when you grow up. Be an asset to your country."

The boys were disappointed. On the way home they discussed why he looked like a spy.

"We were lucky that he wasn't really a spy," Adam stated. "If he was we could have been trapped. He would have killed us if he had thought we knew. The lady might have locked the front door and we would have never got out alive."

The boys were relieved as well. There was a brief discussion about the possibility of the man being a spy AND working for the government. Somehow it was easier to accept that the man was what he said he was, or better yet, what his wife said he was.

"The proof," Charles said, "may be that spies look like people who are not spies. Our man looked like a spy, thus he could not have been one." The boys digested this profound statement and concluded that he was not a spy because he worked for the Government. Charles would get to tell Mary Anne the bad news the next day.

Winter

Chapter Nineteen

Turning Ten

harles had a birthday party and the gang was there. He was now ten years old and very happy. Somehow, he had managed to solve many problems in the past year. He was surrounded by friends and family. There were presents of books, clothes and a crow game with spring-loaded gun to knock the crows over with. Merle gave him a big bag of marbles. The best present of all was a very heavy hunting knife from Canada. It was ground down from a file and guaranteed by Robert never to break. The holster was hand-made, too—from cowhide. Rose promptly took the knife and promised safekeeping for Charles until he would be old enough to use it.

Mary Anne gave him a hug and a pair of woolen mittens she had knitted for him.

"Don't make snowballs with them. They will get wet and ruined. They're to keep your hands warm."

There were cookies with ice cream and cake. Everybody had a good time. After the party Rose took Charles aside.

"I heard what you did to the bully at school. Mary Anne told me." Rose shook her head and smiled. "I feel sorry for anybody who crosses you. Today you're a year older. You're growing up to be a fine young boy. Sometimes you act older than your age. I see you very much like your father. He's a man of great physical strength and courage. That's why I love him so. I also see much of my father in you. Someday we'll go to visit my folks in Canada and you'll see where you get some of your cleverness."

She hugged him knowing the puzzled look on his face was an excuse to hide his ability to digest what she told him. He was a boy of few words—like his mother. She remembered the tricks and tactics she used to separate Tom from the girls he had when she first met him. She played hard to get while working behind the lines to keep the other girls at a respectable distance. Once when she found out he was going away on a Sunday with another girl, she went out into the equipment shed and ripped some wires out of a tractor. She called on him on late Saturday afternoon and insisted that he come out that next day to fix it or he would lose her father's business.

Before Adam left he had asked Charles if they could go on a trip with the gang before the weather got too cold and the snow fell. Charles thought it would be a good idea. A plan was proposed for the coming Saturday.

That Saturday Charles skipped the movies to go off with the gang. They started out at the waterfall, where Richard stopped to drink the water.

"Don't drink it!" Charles warned. "Mrs. Boothby said it was full of germs." Charles had remembered her disclosing the amoebas hiding in the free water.

"That's stupid." Richard said as he drank. The other boys also drank. Charles didn't know who was right. He decided to wait and see if the boys got sick afterward. He knew he didn't get sick when he drank there before but he wasn't sure if anything had changed.

The boys charged over the hills and rock walls. They ran around the briar patch hoping to scare a rabbit out but nothing moved. Adam threw rocks into it and still nothing came out. They went on. Finally, they found the narrow dirt road between the blueberry bush hills. They followed until it stopped at a large farmhouse with a big barn behind it. Behind the house the hills ended and a large pasture began. Cows grazed in the pasture. The boys advanced to investigate.

There did not appear to be anybody home at the farm. The boys walked undisturbed along the rail fence. The closest cows looked up at them and continued eating from a pile of hay near the fence. Merle spotted something interesting.

"Look what I found!" he exclaimed as he ran along the fence. They followed him until he stopped. A dead cow lay in the middle of the pasture. The animal was bloated. It lay on its back grotesquely inflated with its feet stuck up in the air. The boys watched as Adam charged into the field with a stick. He was going to poke it to see if it would move, blow up, or do something he hadn't thought of yet. He got halfway out to the dead critter when there was a loud snort from the group of feeding animals. One of the animals started running towards the boy. Adam dropped his stick and headed back for the fence. He dove through it as the other boys laughed loudly over his retreat.

They wandered over to the big barn. The boys went through the open doors. There was light in the middle of the open door and windows below the eaves. The rest of the barn was dark. The boys gingerly walked down the middle aisle. There were stalls on each side where animals were tethered to the walls. Their hindquarters were exposed to the boys in the open aisle. The barn smelled strongly of urine and dung. Charles went up to a stall. A large black bull raised his head and snorted loudly. He was held by a ring through his nose with a rope through it. His nostrils flared as fierce large dark eyes stared back at Charles. The noise was startling. The bull looked very mean and unhappy. Charles headed back to the open door. Before he got there a farmer appeared from nowhere in response to the noise.

"Hey! What are you boys doing in there!" he yelled at the top of his voice. He appeared as cross and unhappy as the bull Charles had just visited. The boys started running out of the barn. The farmer made no attempt to stop them, but just stood there looking mean and angry as the children ran past him and down the dirt road.

The boys regrouped out of sight of the farm.

"Wow!" Adam exclaimed. "I'm sure glad to get away from that place."

"Me, too," Merle remarked.

They marched home with the understanding they would not say a word to their parents about the adventure.

That evening Rose read to Charles from the Bible. He was growing up and she wanted him to become aware of the changes that he would undergo as he wended his way through life. She opened to Ecclesiastes, Chapter 3:

"Charles," she said, "I want to read a passage from the Bible to give you something to think about. Now that you're ten years old you are not my little boy anymore." She started reading slowly so he would grasp the meaning of the statement.

"This section of the Bible discusses the meaning of life. The part I'm reading to you concerns the changes of times in life. As you know, Charles, everything is always changing. Nobody can stop the changes. They must be understood and recognized. Listen carefully to what the Bible has to say about it." Rose cleared her throat and began reading.

"To everything there is a season, and a time to every purpose under the heaven: A time to be born, and a time to die; a time to plant, and a time to pluck up that which is planted; a time to kill, and a time to heal; a time to break down, and a time to build up; a time to weep, and a time to laugh; a time to mourn, and a time to dance; a time to cast away stones, and a time to gather stones together; a time to embrace, and a time to refrain from embracing; a time to get, and a time to lose; a time to keep, and a time to cast away; a time to rend, and a time to sew; a time to keep silence, and a time to speak; a time to love, and a time to hate; a time of war, and a time of peace." Rose paused for a minute.

"Charles, that section of the Bible has all the wisdom of life in it. Be aware that people have lived out a whole lifetime without understanding the simple message in that passage."

Charles thought for a minute about the truth in the statement.

"Is the Bible saying that everything has its own time and will change and there is a good and bad side to everything that happens?"

"That's true, Charles. In life there will be good times and bad times. There will be feasts and famines. Be aware of the changes and accept them. When you're in good health or having a good time be aware that it is good and that it can change. Now before you go to sleep, think about what I read tonight."

Charles lay awake thinking about the statements that his mother had made. He was lucky to have good health and to have a good home. I was lucky I didn't get killed in Canada, he thought. What the Bible said was that there are both good and bad times in life. That was my bad time. He thought back to the terrible feeling he had when he heard the wind in the pines before the accident. He had never known fear before that, except in the dream he had before the hunting expedition.

The terror of the accident came back to him as he lay in bed. The pain, cold, hunger, loneliness, and fear returned to his thoughts from where he had hidden them since the long journey down the mountain. He refrained from talking to people about the accident because he wanted to keep the memory concealed as deeply in his mind as possible. Now the accident and journey from the mountain refused to stay buried. He reviewed the events as vividly as if they were on a movie screen in front of him. The knot of fear returned to his stomach.

Charles reached inside his mind for his metric clock. He drifted off into the wilderness again but now the pain was distant. Instead, he experienced a magic carpet that took over where gravity failed him. He was wading through the water with his burden on his back, while his whole body was numb to the present. He plodded on hour after hour with no feelings or desires. Finally, he reached the ocean road and his life returned to him. And the pain, exhaustion and hunger didn't hurt as he faded into sleep.

Chapter Twenty

Gang War Again

Winter came with a vengeance. The Thanksgiving holidays had barely ended when bitter cold gripped the countryside. Tom shut the hose water off inside the cellar so that it would not freeze and burst the outside pipes. The walk to school became an ordeal with zero temperatures and winds to face. The children did not go outside very much. A warm fire at home was the most desirable asset in the world.

Charles would come home from school and slide under the cast-iron stove with his head and shoulders sticking out. This was one of the few advantages of being small for his age. He would read his books on the linoleum floor if nobody complained. After his tail had warmed up he would move to the kitchen table.

One particularly cold morning Charles and Mary Anne were hurrying to get to school in the shortest time. Small clouds of steam formed when they breathed through the scarves they held over their faces. They passed the waterfall. The creek was frozen solid.

"Maybe the waterfall is frozen too," Charles commented as they hurried on their way. "Will you go there with me after school to see?" he asked.

Mary Anne hated the cold more than Charles, but she was also curious.

"I'll go if it's warmer out," she replied.

After school Charles left his books home and went directly to her house. He didn't want to get comfortable before going out in the cold again. Mary Anne came to the door all bundled up with just her eyes and pigtails showing. They hurried off to the creek.

The creek was indeed frozen solid. Charles jumped on it and the ice did not break. There was no water underneath. They slid and walked on the ice until they came to the waterfall. The pool under it was solid ice. The ice was clouded because of the way it had frozen. The waterfall stood suspended in space.

"Wow, look at that!" Charles exclaimed.

The water had gradually formed an ice stalagmite at the pool where some of it had frozen before it could all run off. Slowly the ice had formed in layers at higher and higher levels until the mass was jutting into the air. The top of the waterfall had frozen downward in the same manner forming a stalactite off the rock wall. An icicle of frozen water stood between the pyramids.

"I'll bet it'll make a heck of a noise when it melts and crashes," Charles commented.

"It's lovely," Mary Anne said. "I never believed the little creek could look so beautiful." She sat down on the creek. Charles sat down next to her.

He felt good being with her at this place. Charles was happy they could share it together. He felt at peace with himself and nature.

"Mary Anne, you know we'll probably never see this sight again as long as we live."

She looked at him in confirmation.

"If I were here alone I wouldn't enjoy it half as much," Charles stated. "Being here with you is what makes me happy."

Mary Anne was silent for a moment. She was happy to be with Charles and her eyes had a feast to enjoy before the cold would make them move on. She did not think the waterfall would stay frozen many days because she had never heard of it being frozen before.

"I'm always happy to come here with you, Charles. Remember the buttercup field? There's always something beautiful for us away from the school and the town. I hope nothing ever changes the places we go to." She said no more because her mother had mentioned that in time the whole area would be full of houses and the country would become a small city on the edge of the marsh.

"This place where we live may change but I'll always be able to close my eyes and remember it like it is now when I use my metric time," Charles said knowing that only he would ever understand what he was talking about.

On the way home Charles kissed her cold cheek briefly. Mary Anne giggled shyly and they continued home with mittened hands clasped. As Charles reached his house he was aware that whatever he saw today would have to last a lifetime. He had seen the signs of change on the way to school and knew the passage of time was irreversible and that he was seeing the best his small corner of the universe had to offer before it would be destroyed forever.

The next day Charles found out his sister was going ice skating on the pond where they had gone fishing with one of her boyfriends. June was going there with her steady boyfriend. After some lively discussion, Rose convinced her to take Charles along with her. When her boyfriend, Roger, showed up, he was very unhappy to have other company. As a result, Charles ended up riding in the rumble seat of the little 1936 Dodge coupe. When they got to the pond Charles was frozen stiff. Even though Charles was cold and could not skate, he was glad that he had come.

The pond was covered with ice skaters. Charles remembered a scene like it in a Charles Dickens novel. Some people brought firewood and were standing around fires on the banks. There were hundreds of happy people skating or standing about enjoying themselves. Small children ran after their parents as they skated around the pond. It was very cold and everybody was wrapped up in scarves, coats, woolen hats, and other clothes, making them look bloated and fat as they moved around on the ice.

The afternoon passed swiftly and suddenly it was dark with light only from the fires at the edge of the pond. The crowd thinned as people got tired and cold. June and Roger were in no hurry to leave. They kept far away from Charles remaining hidden in the crowd or the depths of the darkness. After a long cold period they appeared from nowhere and bundled Charles back in the rumble seat with a blanket to return home.

The snow came. At first it gently blanketed the hills and streets with a welcomed change from the continuous cold winter days. The pureness of the snow on the hillsides was a visual feast for people to enjoy. Soon, however, the snow melted turning to ice and slush. Then it snowed again. This time it came with an icy wind and the storm lasted for days. When it was over, the countryside was changed. The streets and hills had taken new forms in drifts and winnowing from rooftops. Fine powder snow was three feet deep on level ground. The drifts were twice as high in places. This storm would not be gone in a day or a week. It would still be there a week later when the next one came along and deposited an equal amount of frozen crystals over the crusty and dirty original lot.

One day in mid-December Merle arrived at Charles' house after school.

"Remember the snowfort we never built?" Merle asked. He was referring to the day when there were not enough kids available to build a good fort and they ended snowballing the shed instead.

Charles nodded and his eyes lit up.

"Gosh, do you think we could make a snowfort now?" he asked.

"Why not. There's lots of snow and it won't melt away before we can finish." Merle, like Charles, had never had an opportunity to build a good snowfort. His greatest effort produced only a snowman on his front lawn.

"Where can we build it?" Charles asked.

Merle had already thought it over.

"Let's build a giant fort across the dead-end street where we had the apple fight. Then we can have a war with the Baker Street gang again."

"Do you mean for the Baker Street gang to make their own fort?" The lights were really shining in the boys' eyes now.

"Sure! Let's meet with the rest of the gang and see if they'll do it."

Merle led the way down the street and by the end of the day, with the gang's approval, he and Charles were looking for Jack on Baker Street.

Jack was throwing snowballs at Margaret, and several other Baker Street female victims he caught by surprise. The girls were relieved to see Merle and Charles. When the boys mentioned the snowfort idea to Jack, they quickly escaped.

The three boys walked down to the end of the street. Jack wanted to build his fort at the end of the street where the barricade was before.

"No sir," Charles said. "That means we have to build our fort in the middle of the street where it'll be in the way of the snowplows or cars. We have to build them on opposite sides of the street."

Jack thought for a minute. He liked the idea. The apple war had been fun. A snowfight would be more fun.

"I'll talk to my gang and get back to you tomorrow."

The next day a lieutenant from the Baker Street gang arrived at Charles' house to inform him that the deal was on. The date of the fight would be set after the forts were finished.

Building the fort was slow hard work. The Marsh Street Gang started out with shovels to get the base established quickly. The snow was still dry and would not pack at all. After a few days they found that they could skim the top few inches of snow off the untrampled areas and get a good sun-warmed layer that would pack.

The Baker Street gang was not missing any tricks. By the end of the third day, all of the snow had been skimmed off the pack halfway down the street, including people's lawns. Every night the cold and tired children would go home and crawl into a warm place to forget what they had been doing all afternoon. The forts grew slowly and started to take form.

A common rule had been established concerning the construction. There was to be no wood or other reinforcement used in the fort. Boards or cardboard could be used to shape the walls or windows but they had to be removed when the fort was finished. The forts would be made from nothing but snow. Thus, the forts grew with the help of boxes to shape windows and not much else. After a week the forts were done. By this time each gang had inspected the other's fort and they ended up looking pretty much the same. They were both four feet high with walls starting two feet thick at the base and narrowing to one foot at the top. The Marsh Street fort had a doorway on the side and three windows in the front. The Baker Street fort had an entrance on the opposite side and two windows in the front. They were both about ten feet square on each side.

An engagement date was set for the following Saturday, only three days away. On Friday the Marsh Street gang was filling boxes with snowballs. The snow in the fort area had all been consumed so they would need to bring their own ammunition to the battle. They filled their wagons again with boxes of snowballs instead of apples. They were stored in Adam's backyard for the battle. They did not dare put them in the fort where they could be stolen by the other gang. His dog Rex would make enough noise, by barking from his back-porch home, to keep intruders away if the Baker Street gang decided to sabotage their supply.

The next morning, they arrived at the war zone with their wagons in tow. When they got inside the fort they found little room to move because of the wagons and boxes of snowballs. Two wagons were unloaded and turned upside down so the boys could stand on them and throw snowballs over the top of the fort. The Baker Street gang arrived shortly afterward. One of them had a wheelbarrow full of snowballs, the other boys used their Red Flier wagons much the same as the competition.

Jack yelled, "Murder the Marsh Street Gang!" and the battle was on. Snowballs flew all around for the first furious minutes. Richard got hit on the head with one from the other side and yelped with pain. He picked it up and showed it to Merle. It was covered with ice. The Baker Street gang had watered them down the night before.

Richard was mad.

He yelled, "You dirty rats! Your snowballs are iced! That's not fair!" to the other side.

A highly predictable answer of:

"That's tough, isn't it!" came from the other fort. The Baker Street gang laughed as loud as they could.

Charles and the other boys had a conference. They were well protected by the fort. The only way they could get hurt was by being careless and getting exposed. They would have to be very careful. It was important not to run out of ammunition before the other side or they would get rushed.

"Meanwhile," Charles suggested, "let's save up their icy ones and when they run out of ammunition we can nail them with their own bad news."

The battle resumed. The Baker Street gang was aggressive and put out a deluge of snowballs. The Marsh Street gang was on the defensive, spending most of the time ducking the iceballs and being careful about returning the fire. Merle stacked the icy ones neatly in a row across the floor of the fort at the back wall. Those were the reserves.

After an hour the battle slowed down. Both sides were getting tired. The cold had not had any effect yet because they were so busy. The Baker Street boys now started venturing outside the fort to scour snow for snowballs. It made lousy ammunition because it would not pack right. It was too dry for snowballs. The Marsh Street boys would concentrate their fire on the outsiders, making it a real run for the money to venture outside the safety of the fort.

The Marsh Street gang ran out of conventional snowballs. The Baker fort had been inactive for a few minutes.

"What do you think is happening?" Adam asked Charles.

"I think they're going to rush us because they're out of ammo and have been scraping the snow off the fort," he answered. He had just watched Adam pelt an arm that reached out a window to scour snow off the front where the snowballs had adhered to the walls.

A moment later the Baker gang came out of the fort screaming their favorite Rebel yell and carrying armloads of snowballs. The Marsh gang plastered them with the icy snowballs. They stopped short in surprise. The icy ones hurt while theirs were falling apart. They retreated and called for an end to the war. Everybody was tired with the evening cold being felt for the first time. The war ended. The boys retired to the rear lines of home pulling their wagons over the snow behind them. There were bruises from the icy snowballs but no other injuries. Another war had ended with no real casualties. Everybody was a winner.

Chapter
Twenty-One

Holidays

Christmas was a welcome respite from school. The children were restless as the holiday season approached. They would look forward to the classroom in the mornings as a refuge from the cold. By afternoon, however, they were anxious to be away. The greatest asset of the holiday season was that it was a change from home and school. It was a chance to get involved in a new activity. The religious significance was not lost on the children who went to church regularly. The other children would enjoy a vacation without knowing the real meaning of the reason for the holidays.

The new teacher, Mrs. Boothby, was as conscientious as Miss Pritchett used to be. She didn't want the Christmas holidays to be a week off from school without any purpose. Her method of teaching on this last Friday before vacation was for the class to sing Christmas carols in class. Then she would have the students discuss the words and meanings of the songs. After the carols were sung and discussed, the class had a party with cake and they exchanged presents. Finally the cheerful, chattering mob was released for the holidays.

On the way home from school the last day before the holidays, Charles was in an argumentative mood.

"Mary Anne, do you think that everybody is both good and bad? I mean that people can be good sometimes and bad at other times?"

"I don't know what you mean. I know everybody does bad things sometimes like smoking, but that doesn't mean they are really bad."

"What if somebody made a law making it bad to hold hands. Is it really bad because someone made the law?"

"I don't understand you. Please don't talk like that." Mary Anne was getting confused with Charles' argument. She did not want to be led into a discussion of things not taught in school.

Charles let the discussion drop. He was beginning to believe that everybody had good and bad in them. The bully was bad to hit him and he was bad to make the slingshot to use on him. Mrs. Boothby was bad to keep him after school and he was bad to put the rats in her car. 'Nobody was perfect,' he thought. 'No wonder they killed Christ. He didn't fight back. They must have killed him because he was perfect. If he wasn't perfect he would have fought back and been bad but alive.' Charles reasoned that he himself was not perfect and was a survivor because he was a fighter.

Charles enjoyed thinking about religious things and creating mental arguments about good versus bad. 'These things don't really have solutions,' he thought. He wondered if he liked to think about them because of his mother's influence. Rose had told Charles when her father quit the farm he put his energies into being a minister. Her father had always been quoting the Bible to her when she lived at home. It ultimately became the educated man's way of life. 'What would it be like to become a preacher when I grow up?' Charles wondered. 'Maybe religious people can answer the questions I have about things. Maybe a person needs to be a minister to find out how things really work in this complicated world. If there really are answers to everything then I would need to be a minister to find out.'

The Christmas season was a good one for Charles. He went to the library and took out a half-dozen books. He liked the Sherlock Holmes novels. They were complicated but fun to read. The weather outside was cold. He did not venture out any more than he had to. The snow war had cured his appetite for outside sports for the month. Christmas Eve finally arrived. June played the piano and they all sang songs. Her latest romance with Roger was over. He was a nice guy but treated his sister as if he had bought her. 'Should anybody own a girlfriend?' Charles asked himself.

There were visits from a few relatives who lived close by, but most of them were far away in Canada and got no closer than the telephone or mail could bring them.

Tom had brought a huge block of chocolate home. It was over an inch thick and must have weighed ten pounds. It was also as hard as a rock. Everybody was trying to whack pieces off it with a big knife. There were more good things to eat that were generally not present except at Thanksgiving—like mincemeat pies, nuts, candy, and home-made chocolate chip cookies. A Christmas tree, trimmed with shiny tin tinsel strips, handmade ornaments, brilliantly colored glass bulbs, and popcorn strung by Charles and his mother, stood in the living room corner. Finally it was bedtime. Charles slept a fitful sleep and woke up early. He was the first one up and opened his presents before anybody else came downstairs.

He received a new sled and red wagon to replace the one that got so much use during the year. There were also books from his friends and neighbors. Mary Anne had knitted him a woolen cap to go with the mittens. He gave her some new card and dice games in return. June received a new bicycle with a wicker basket to replace the one she had used for five years. Her ex-boyfriend, Roger, arrived later on with a gold ring for her present and June surprised everybody by accepting it and making up with him.

A few days later a small box arrived for Charles by mail from Canada. He hastily opened it and found a gold-filled pocket watch inside. There was a note enclosed from Uncle Ralph. "Dear Charles," it read. "Please accept this small gift for saving my son last September. I hope you will always be able to use your time as well as you did then. Robert and I are forever grateful. Happy holidays, Uncle Ralph."

Charles studied the engraving of a hunting scene on the cover and back. It was a beautiful scene with a hunter raising his shotgun as his dog pointed to a pheasant taking flight. Then he opened the case and admired the ivory face and gunblue hands. He also took the back off and studied the bright steel frame and spinning gears. He wound and set it from the kitchen clock. For days he showed it to everybody he met. Nothing made him smile as much as the watch did. After all, time was awfully important to Charles.

The holidays continued as a large snowstorm blotted out the landscape for several days. When it was over, a hilly street had been blocked off with people leaving their cars at the bottom. All the children in the neighborhood, including Charles, headed that way with their sleds. For one glorious afternoon the children tore down the hill on their new and old sleds and trudged up the hill afterward. A procession of happy children formed a speeding track down the hill and a slow procession back. At the end of the day the snowplow arrived and the game ended. It was time to go home.

At year-end Charles made the rounds of the trash cans one evening before the rubbish men were to empty them. He collected all the Christmas trees he could find. When he got home he lined them up around the perimeter of the grape arbor that surrounded the back side of the house. When he finished he counted twenty-five trees. They made an effective wall. This was his new winter fort. He couldn't find much use for the new fort because it was outside where it was always cold. He couldn't light a candle in there either because the dry trees were so hazardous. One day his mother ordered them to be put out into the street because they were such a fire hazard and eyesore. The Trashmen were very surprised to find the twenty-five Christmas trees sitting on the curb for them at the end of January.

School had started again and, after a long dearth of holidays, Valentine's Day was the only coming event. It was not a school holiday but the children looked forward to it because it was a welcome break from the daily routine. Everyone in the class had bought the five-and-dime store Valentines that had to be cut out of big paper books and folded together. It kept the children busy for the week. Everybody gave Valentines to their friends in class. It was great to receive these simple presents from the other children. There was one in particular that Charles liked. It was a big one from Mary Anne. She created it from the cutout pages. There was a knight on a white horse in the picture. He held a long jousting lance in his hand. Inside the fold the card read "I love you forever, Mary Anne."

Charles looked over at the simple blonde girl who was looking back at him. His heart filled with joy. He smiled at her with the knowledge that he loved her today and would always. She always made him feel happy inside. He could worry about things and think about the world but somehow it was important to his being that she was always close by. There was permanent room in his heart for her, next to his family and the gang. Charles knew forever was never any further away than tomorrow. He also knew he was the master of his own time. He opened the case of his gold pocket watch. It was 10:59; there were almost 41 minutes left in his hour.

The Metric Clock:

Postlude

It was Sunday morning...still early because frost coated the grass on the lawn. They left in a large car driven by a parishioner. Charles had not been feeling well since breakfast.

"I don't feel well, but it doesn't matter because today is such a bright clear day," he told Mary Anne. But it did matter because it made his strength disappear and left him feeling weak and tired.

Mary Anne had asked the driver to pick them up an hour early to bring Charles and her to the Church. This would give them half an hour to spare, so they wouldn't need to rush. As they approached the Church Charles asked the driver to keep driving on. They passed it when Charles told him:

"I'll tell you when to stop."

"We're going to be late for Church," Mary Anne stated. She was always one to question and correct his course like a helmsman navigating a great ship at sea.

Charles took an old pocket watch from his jacket pocket. The gold plate had been worn off the highlights of an engraved hunting scene, exposing the brass case. He opened it looking at the time while subconsciously winding it.

"There's time to go. I want to visit the fishpond where the Gang caught the giant goldfish." A thin smile creased Charles's face as he anticipated the stop.

They drove on until a tall stone wall loomed up on the left.

"Drive in the cemetery gate on the left when you see it," Charles instructed the driver.

"You're not dead yet," the driver joked lightly as he looked back grinning.

Charles smiled at him.

"Please drive to the rear of the cemetery. When I was a boy I went fishing in a pond there. I want to see it again if I can.

They turned through open wrought iron gates following a road around orderly rows of tombstones protruding from an endless manicured lawn shaded by large trees. The narrow road then passed through an area with no headstones and stopped at a wrought iron fence which stretched across the cemetery from one side to the other. When the car stopped Charles slowly got out and walked up to the gate. He gazed at a small pond sheltered by bushes and mature elm trees which shaded the benches and paths that wound around it. His heart pounded with excitement.

"Mary Anne, come here! The pond is unchanged. It seems smaller but just like before when we were here. And the trees are bigger."

Mary Anne and the driver came up to the fence. "It's beautiful!" she exclaimed. "Just as you said it was."

Charles pointed to a row of bushes on the opposite side.

"That's where we caught the fish. The giant goldfish. I think it was Adam who caught it. What a day that was!" Charles was all smiles now, finding part of his past intact. "You know, Mary Anne, the only thing we have found unchanged since we returned, has been kept intact by a Church. Doesn't that reinforce my conviction that the Church, all Churches, are the keepers of the past. The preservers of our fate."

Mary Anne said nothing. 'I'm happy that he's able to forget his pain and sickness by finding a part of his past not erased by the changes of time,' she thought, squeezing his hand. 'It's so good to share some happiness with him again after making the long journey back home. Sometimes I regret that I cannot share his pain.' She had not realized that she had felt his pain without sharing his illness.

For half an hour they watched the ducks cruise the pond and listened to the birds, which flitted back and forth from skeletal boughs.

"They should have gone south by now," Charles commented as the blue and grey mallards swam close by the shore.

"Maybe they waited for you to visit." Mary Anne quipped.

Their driver pointed to his watch and a minute later they left for the Church. A colorfully dressed large crowd had gathered outside. When Charles got out they surged forward amid a babble of voices. He was led inside to a seat in the front row as the crowd followed. After many introductions the noise quieted down when the pastor left Charles for the lectern. His talk was an accolade to Charles' past and accomplishments in the Church. He finished his speech with an introduction for Charles to speak for a few minutes. As Charles approached the lectern the pastor reminded the congregation that Charles had been ill and not to make unreasonable demands on his time and strength.

Charles refused the robe of his office when he first arrived and now stood in front of the filled Church in his loosely-fitting dark suit. Strong lights made his prematurely white hair shine eerily. The man who had become a powerful voice of the Church was now standing fragile and weak behind the lectern. His slender body was partly concealed but his thin voice evidenced his illness. He cleared his throat and began.

"I want to thank everybody here for your kindness and an opportunity to return to my humble beginnings in this town and in this very Church. I believe that if I hadn't had my start in life here I probably wouldn't have had the desire to accomplish my goals and good for the Church. My dearest memories are from this town and its people. That's why I am here today. I'm pleased that I've been allowed to carry out my life-long philosophy that the Church, these granite-walled institutions," he lifted his arm and pointed to the arched stone-walled annex to the clerestory on his left, "are the jewel boxes that safely hold the people and the Lord inside. It's always been my goal to let the Church become the keeper of the treasures of our Lord and not to dictate how people should live and act. Within this framework the Church, our Church, has grown with a divine strength and purpose over the years. The independence and guidance of this institution have been its strength and salvation. You and I will pass on but this Church will preserve, through the decades and centuries, the ideals that have brought all of us together under this roof."

Charles coughed a prolonged cough, and continued weaker than before.

"I will close with the thought that the goal of this Church, and of all Churches, is to help us become better people while we pass our short time on His earth." After a pause he concluded with a large smile, "Thanks for your hospitality. It's meant a lot to this tired old man. I'll need to live at least a millennium to read all of those wonderful books that you left me."

He stepped back from the lectern as the audience stood up clapping loudly. Charles sat down while the clapping continued to fill the Church. For several minutes he and Mary Anne were the only people sitting. He felt weak and flushed with joy. Grasping Mary Anne's hand, he saw tears in her eyes. Charles dug a handkerchief from his pocket and gave it to her. Suddenly he could not see from tears welling up in his own eyes. His composure dissolved. A hidden emotional artery had been severed. Decades of feeling gushed from his soul and he began to cry like a child. He had not wanted to give a sermon but simply to say goodbye to his townsmen.

Charles went to bed early that evening. Dinner was passed by; he had not been able to keep any food down. He was tired as never before. The day had been pleasant and rewarding beyond expectation but it left him exhausted. Emotionally he was drained. The morning at Church had pulled the plug on a lifetime of dormant and pent-up feelings. As soon as he lay down he went to sleep.

In his pained and troubled sleep, he began to dream of his youth and the screaming, yelling group of children gathered around a large goldfish at the forbidden fishpond. Suddenly he had a vision of the clock of life that he had not seen for forty years. The large hand represented his life as it moved around the face. When the hand neared the top, he recognized the fragile worn-out person that he had become. His pain ceased.

A profusion of bright yellow gold and buttercup fragrance filled the ground, dancing in the breeze. There was a feeling of spring in the warm dancing sun, of sugar sap rushing skyward in maples, leaf buds unfurling explosively from barren branches, and pitch gushing from cracks and crevices in the pines. Flights of sparrows flew overhead in noisy celebration. Charles was sitting in the golden field, a soft radiance surrounded him, but he was not alone. His Maker was there beside him. They were waiting for Mary Anne to join them. It would not be long.

THE END

About the Author

*P*hillip **Bruce Chute, EA** is a businessman-writer. He is currently a tax and financial advisor with a consulting practice in Temecula, California. He has been an Enrolled Agent of the U.S. Treasury since 1976.

Phil served as a paratrooper in the 82nd Airborne Division in the States and Europe during the Cold War. His ancestry dates back to warrior-king Robert Bruce of Scotland and the Speaker of Parliament Chaloner Chute of England. There have also been many Phillip Chute Members of Parliament in England since Phillip Chute, the standard bearer at the Battle of Boulogne, saved the life of King Henry V111. The famous king rewarded Phillip with a lion for his family coat of arms, a castle, and the sapphire from his ring.

Both the Bruce and the Chute families date back to time of the Battle of Hastings with William the Conqueror in 1066.

This is Phillip's first children's book but he has several other published works including *Silver Thread of Life*, *Rock and Roll Murders*, and *American Independent Business*. He is also completing several other novels currently. As a writer, Phillip has won National and International awards from Kiwanis International. He has also published articles for the *Nova Scotia* periodical, *The Shore News*, and been interviewed by *Entrepreneur* Magazine.

Phillip Chute lives in Temecula, CA with Nanette Lariosa, a retired educator. Both work out of their home. They also enjoy their many grandchildren and two rambunctious Labrador mixed dogs.

The Author's Other Works

American Independent Business: His first book sold 5,000 copies and was used as a college textbook and reference for business entrepreneurs and he's hard at work on a second version.

Rock & Roll Murders: Fiction, based on a true story about the KOLA radio station-Fred Cote Murder-One trials and conviction in Riverside of 1990.

The Silver Thread of Life: Real accounts of spiritual encounters by the author and others.

Stocks Bonds and Entrepreneurs: Based on the authors 20 years as Securities Representative, Registered Principal OSJ, and Registered Investment Advisor. The material is provided by the author's investment client experience and by thousands of his tax clients. - coming 12/2018 in e-book

Trust Me: Based on a True Story of a conman-coming 2019

Hazardous Business: Fictional Story-coming 2019